Kensington Books by Davis Bunn

Miramar Bay
Firefly Cove
Moondust Lake
Tranquility Falls
The Cottage on Lighthouse Lane
The Emerald Tide
Shell Beach
Midnight Harbor

Novellas
The Christmas Hummingbird
The Christmas Cottage

THE CHRISTMAS COTTAGE

THE CHRISTMAS COTTAGE

DAVIS BUNN

KENSINGTON
PUBLISHING CORP.

www.kensingtonbooks.com

KENSINGTON BOOKS are published by

Kensington Publishing Corp.
900 Third Avenue
New York, NY 10022

All Kensington titles, imprints and distributed lines are available at special quantity discounts for bulk purchases for sales promotion, premiums, fund-raising, educational or institutional use. Special book excerpts or customized printings can also be created to fit specific needs. For details, write or phone the office of the Kensington Special Sales Manager: Kensington Publishing Corp., 900 Third Avenue, New York, NY, 10022. Attn. Special Sales Department. Phone: 1-800-221-2647.

The K with book logo Reg. U.S. Pat. & TM Off.

Library of Congress Control Number: 2024936515

ISBN: 978-1-4967-4832-4

First Kensington Hardcover Edition: October 2024

ISBN: 978-1-4967-4833-1 (ebook)

10 9 8 7 6 5 4 3 2 1

Printed in the United States of America

THE CHRISTMAS COTTAGE

1

Olivia needed two and a half days to drive from Los Angeles to Miramar. Part of it came down to the pre-Christmas traffic. Southern Californian drivers tended to go nuts in bad weather. There was no logic to it, so theories abounded. Olivia doubted it was actually aliens losing contact with their control subjects when clouds blanketed the region. More than likely it was because storms robbed the journey of any possible pleasure. Under conditions like these, cold and wet and windy and dark and gray, travelers were desperate to get the trip over and done.

But mostly her slow pace was because of the roads. She had of course heard about the storms that had lumbered off the Pacific, hurricane-force winds and weeks of torrential downpour. But LA had been spared the worst, and her own world had become reduced to making it through tempests of a more personal nature.

Once she passed Ventura, the true extent of storm damage became very real. Twice the highway was reduced from ten lanes to two by mudslides. Even when the freeway opened back up, the rubble not picked up by the scrapers remained ankle deep in places. Some drivers still insisted on scrambling over the debris fields, spewing gravel at the saner travelers.

Olivia actually found a sullen comfort in the slow progress, the swirling gray blanket overhead, the sudden lashing storms that came and went in seconds. Her mind flickered back and forth over the previous months, like a tongue gingerly probing a broken tooth.

Despite everything that had happened, she couldn't bring herself to call her ex-husband a bad man. Gareth had occasionally thrown himself into situations he regretted afterwards. Typical hormone-driven, adolescent-minded male, was how her city friends called him. But in the good times, and there had been many, those were some of the traits that had made life with Gareth so exciting. They had also fueled Gareth's success as a television producer. He had swept Olivia off her feet, and for five and a half years their romantic moments had left her breathless.

But as Olivia's friends back in Miramar had warned, love in the big city was a roller coaster of a ride.

Seven months back, Gareth had finally confessed

to what Olivia had long suspected. His impetuous nature had drawn him into the arms of a lovely young starlet. Olivia and her soon-to-be ex were still involved in the divorce when Gareth was struck by a trio of blows, bam-bam-bam, lightning fast and fatal. The new flame of his life ran off with a stuntman who claimed he had a real shot at stardom. Then the striking writers and actors froze his projects in development, and he was forced to declare bankruptcy. Which was when he took Olivia to dinner at their former favorite restaurant and confessed he was so broke he couldn't pay his lawyers. Alimony was out of the question.

Five days later, Gareth was felled by a heart attack.

Farewell, wayward lad. Olivia actually cried at his funeral.

Of course, none of this was why it had taken her nine long years to make the return journey to Miramar.

The road from San Luis Obispo was a seventy-mile tale of unnatural events. Rubble and flooded areas reduced the county highway to one lane in places. The drive normally took no more than ninety minutes. Today she needed five and a half hours. When the crawling traffic stopped moving altogether, which was often, people rose from their cars. Stretched.

Olivia did the same. In truth, she was not sorry for the difficult journey. It kept her mind off everything that waited up ahead.

The sky was an artist's pallet of grays. The air tasted wet, thick with rain that did not fall. In the awful days gone by, she had repeatedly turned off the television whenever newscasters referred to the central coast storms. Any mention of her childhood home had Olivia reaching for the remote. She had not bothered with the papers or evening news. Not once in seven long and weary months.

She finally approached Miramar by the light of a sullen dusk. Olivia was tempted to head straight for the seashore walk, which had formed such a vital part of her early years. It was there she had set her course south. Determined to leave the small-town life. Certain her world was bigger than Miramar.

But that walk would have to wait. There were already too many emotions surrounding her return. She needed to be strong when facing that path. Ready for the act of surrender.

Miramar's main street surprised her. A lot. Enough to push aside the recollections, draw her fully into the now.

She drove slowly up Ocean Avenue, aiming for the guesthouse where she had planned to spend her first few nights. Preparing for the hardship of returning home. Now she understood why there had been no response to her emailed requests for a room, nor any answer to her calls. Miramar's main street was lined with an odd assortment of cars. Pickups and SUVs and campers jammed the fire lane and grass verges, something that would never have been permitted in her day.

The guesthouse parking lot was blocked by a pair of sawhorses. Castaways Restaurant was closed. Olivia turned down the side lane leading to the employees' parking lot and found a space. She walked back to Ocean Avenue and stood there. Trying to understand what was happening.

The sidewalks were as full as she'd expect for the season. But the people showed no joy. The children were kept close. No running around or pulling on arms or shouting. And the clothes. Wrinkled, some stained, all of them worse for wear. The scene reminded her of hard-luck times in the farming valleys. People and cars drifting by, going nowhere at a very slow pace.

The guesthouse's sign had a NO VACANCY shingle dangling in the fitful breeze. Olivia stopped halfway up the walk, halted by the handwritten sign taped to the front window: DON'T EVEN ASK.

Olivia crossed the street, climbed one block, and was almost prepared for the sight that greeted her inside the diner, the Ocean Avenue Grill. Every table was taken, every chair. But there was none of the normal chatter. The faces were both weary and unfamiliar. Of course, she had not been back in eight years. Still, she would have expected to recognize somebody. The diner was the center of town gossip, the place where the idlers gathered. . . .

A waitress pushed through the doors, her tray overfull with what appeared to be six identical orders. She froze and gaped. Then called, "You stay right there." She set down the plates, offered one of the children a smile, then hurried over. "Great heavens above. Is that really you?"

"Hello, Claire."

"What on earth are you doing here?"

"Nowhere else to go."

"I've been hearing that tune far too often these days." Claire Levant gripped Olivia's arm with her free hand. "You just come with me."

A number of the children they passed were asleep, either cradled in their parents' arms or using the table for a headrest. Claire pushed through the kitchen doors and announced, "We've got ourselves another hungry stray."

Arnaud Levant, the head cook and Claire's husband, was a rapier-thin man, whose hair was caught in a colorful scarf that matched his pirate's grin. "Wow."

Claire beamed. "I know, right?"

"Hi, Arnaud."

"Olivia, you haven't aged a day."

"Several centuries, more like," she replied. "Where it counts most."

"You always were the honest one," Claire said.

"Correction. You always brought it out in me."

Her two former best friends, now married, did their best to smile. But they saw enough of Olivia's inner state, and struggled as a result. Arnaud asked, "Hungry?"

"Famished. I've been trapped on the road since daybreak."

"We're serving just two dishes today. Stew and stew."

"Don't ask what's inside," Claire said. "Fricasseed gopher, most like."

"Supplies are coming in days late, if at all," Araud agreed. "But I'll fish out the questionable bits."

"Stew sounds great."

Claire led her past the dishwasher's station, back to where a whitewashed ledge jutted between the larder and the rear door. Claire patted a stool and said, "Make yourself comfortable."

"Won't your boss raise a stink, me being back here?"

Claire raised her voice. "Yo, boss? You mind?"

Arnaud called back, "Probably. What about?"

Olivia said, "You're joking."

"The former owner had a heart thing," Claire explained. "We caught him when he fell."

"A heart thing."

"You want specifics, go talk to the doc out front. You know we always wanted our own place."

"Since you two started dating." Her oldest friend was narrower, and gray strands nearly dominated her formerly copper curls. Claire looked ten years older than her real age of thirty-one.

But she was happy. Arnaud too. Their glowing satisfaction, even in the midst of this glum company, gave Olivia a burn at heart level. She asked, "Do you have children?"

"A boy, he's four."

"First of many," Arnaud agreed. "I'm thinking, eleven."

"Not with me you're not." To Olivia, "Arnaud's parents are playing surrogates and loving the duty almost too much."

"They're hoping for twins next go-round," Arnaud offered.

"Different comment, same response," Claire said, then noticed Olivia's reaction. Her gaze softened as she asked, "Girl, what happened?"

But before she could respond, the kitchen's rear door opened and the chief of police declared, "I'll have a steak well done and four eggs fried so hard you can nail them to the wall."

"Not here, you won't," Claire replied.

Arnaud stepped back from the stove far enough to grin at the newcomer. "We've got the tastiest gopher stew in six states."

"Then stew it is." He dropped his hat on the table, then realized who was seated across the table. "Stars above."

"What I said," Claire offered.

"Hello, Porter."

"Olivia, what on earth?"

"My thoughts exactly," Claire said. She patted Olivia's shoulder, silencing her best friend's response. "First the girl eats, then we interrogate."

The stew was, in a word, fabulous. There was of course no gopher. Olivia knew because Claire described how Arnaud grilled cubes of tofu, then slow-cooked a delicate casserole with a marrow base that twice each year he simmered for an entire day. The veggies were all supplied by local hothouse growers.

"Since these two took over, the quality of this place has gone through the roof, sure enough," Porter said.

"Doesn't stop the old-timers from moaning," Claire said. "Loudly."

When the plates were empty and fresh mugs steamed in front of them, Claire said, "Okay, we've been patient long enough."

Olivia asked, "What about all the customers out front?"

"Guess they'll have to starve a while longer," Claire replied. "Bad joke."

"Terrible," Porter agreed. "You should be ashamed."

Claire demanded, "Girl, tell us about life in La-La Land."

"It was great," Olivia said. Somehow it felt okay. Revealing her fresh wounds here. In the company of friends she left behind. People who didn't fit into the dreams she had chased so hard. Not to mention the other reason she didn't come home for so long. "Fabulous. Everything I'd ever wanted for myself and more. Until it wasn't."

Porter said, "So things fell apart."

"Oh no. That doesn't go nearly far enough. What's the name of those missiles they shoot from battleships?"

"From destroyers," Arnaud corrected. He leaned against the tiled wall, listening. "Tomahawks. City killers."

"Those," Olivia said. "A lot of them."

Claire's voice was softened by very real concern. "So that man who swept you away. Took you to the big city. Promised you a lifelong love. I forget his name."

Arnaud offered, "Gareth."

"Him. He left you?"

"Twice."

There was a silence, a sharing of looks, then Porter

said to the others, "Why are you making me be the one to ask?"

"You're the cop," Arnaud replied. "It's your job. Asking the horrible questions."

Porter said, "Olivia, you took the man back?"

"No. Never." She found genuine comfort in how easy this conversation was going. As if she needed to be back here again. After all those years. "I think maybe that was what Gareth wanted. After his lollipop of a fiancée ran off with the stuntman and Gareth's company went bust in the strikes. But my ex never had a chance to ask, on account of how Gareth had a heart attack and died. So that particular request was never uttered. The best thing I can say about that chapter is Gareth's former new flame, Little Ms. Lollipop, didn't show up for his funeral."

Olivia found a distinct comfort in being surrounded by the friends she'd left behind. Watching them struggle to hide their smiles.

Claire managed, "I'm so sorry."

Arnaud said, "No you're not."

"Well, sure I am. Not about the LA louse, though. Him I might never forgive. Even if he is toast." To Olivia, "I'm sorry for all you've been through."

"Thanks. To get it all out in the open, just to round out the sorry tale. That same strike demolished my business. Last month I filed for bankruptcy. I've spent the past five weeks tearing down my life. Selling the house. Watching the lawyers turn my savings into party hats. I haven't watched the news or read a paper since forever. Longer."

Claire's eyes widened. "So you don't know."

The reality was there in their faces. The same dark stain, the concern. All the humor gone now.

Olivia breathed. Tried to ask. But she couldn't. Not with everything that had brought her here. The words just would not come.

Porter Wright slid off the stool, fitted his hat on properly, and offered Olivia his hand. "You just come with me."

A fitful wind pushed them up Ocean Avenue. Rain fine as Pacific mist struck once, twice, then the storm departed. Sort of. The sky went back to swirling gray strands as they passed a family clustered on a sidewalk bench. Porter stopped and indicated the camper parked in a fire zone. He asked the parents, "Is this yours?"

The kids watched in solemn resignation as the father stood. "I'll move it."

"Stay where you are." Porter took out his ticket pad, scribbled, tore off a sheet. "If anyone asks, show them this. We're hoping the northern routes will reopen tomorrow. Three days, tops." He started walking. "Come on, Olivia."

As they continued away from the Pacific, she asked, "Is your daughter coming home for the holidays?"

"Celia's here now. But it looks like she'll be heading back to school soon as the northern roads reopen. She's working on some time-sensitive project and can't risk getting stuck here. Which could well happen if we're trapped by another storm." He glanced at her. "I'd offer you a place. But Celia came down with six friends who couldn't make it up north. Three are in her room, three in the barn. She's sleeping on a pallet in our room. Sorry."

Olivia decided it was time to ask, "What aren't you telling me?"

The chief stopped and removed his hat and stood as solemn as a funeral director. "Olivia, honey, you're not going home. Not tonight, not tomorrow. Maybe in a while. But I wouldn't count on it happening anytime soon."

"Mom's cottage . . . It's gone?"

"Not entirely. The cottage's foundations have held. Mostly." He replaced his hat. Giving his hands something to do. "You'll need to have an expert make a careful inspection once the valley roads reopen."

She had no idea what to say. Porter nodded, as if her silence was the proper response.

He touched her arm, guiding her around and on up Ocean Avenue. "We've lost more than half the seafront walk. These folks you see, they were evacuated from the oceanfront hotels. The ones from down south are crawling home. These others . . ."

"Porter, where are you taking me?"

"Only place in town with a free bed." He started them down the side street leading to the police station. "Where are you parked?"

"In the employee lot behind Castaways."

"Once you're settled, bring your car over here. Tell Maud I said it was okay."

She halted outside the station doors. "You're putting me inside the jail?"

"Don't knock it. This is restricted to locals only. I've had outsiders offer me five hundred dollars for a cell." He held the door open, waved her inside. "Come on, I've got to go make sure Miramar stays crime-free. Don't know what we'd do if we nabbed a felon. Cuff him to the fence, I suppose."

"I actually don't know what to say."

He ushered her inside. "Yeah, I get a lot of that these days."

2

Dillon Farrow's first day back in Miramar was spent mopping jail cells.

He had returned any number of times, mostly brief holiday stays with his grandparents. Since their passing two years back, though, not once. There was nothing to come back to, no reason to visit the town he had fought so hard to escape.

But there he was, using a mix of dishwasher soap and liquid deodorizer, trying to erase the stench of the police-strength industrial cleaner. Surrounded by families who were mostly grateful for a cell. Wondering if this day could possibly get any worse.

Which was the moment when none other than Olivia Greer came waltzing through the station's front door.

Dillon's knee-jerk response was to jam the mop back into the metal wheelie bucket and roll it down the central corridor. Fast as the little rattling beast would let him.

Hoping desperately that Olivia had not recognized him.

Wishing the jail had a rear fire escape. Unbarred window. Crevice he could crawl into and hide.

He entered the last and largest cell, the drunk tank. It was the only cell not occupied by a family, and for good reason. The windowless chamber defined vile. Cracked discolored tiles covered the floor and walls, rising to a ceiling that gave yellow a bad name. The smell was brutal.

Dillon did his best to lose himself in work. It had been his escape hatch for as long as he could remember. More than that. Dillon actually enjoyed working. Having a task and doing it well defined his best days, even as a child.

He mopped and rinsed and squeezed and mopped. In the process, the woman beyond the steel door receded as other memories rose up and took form.

The best one-word description of Dillon's parents was, *stoned*.

Dillon's early years had been defined by the stoner's version of a dream world. His parents had seen themselves as sixties flower children born a generation too late. These would-be hipsters baked dope into their breakfast granola, grew marijuana in their veggie garden, and played early rock on scratched and worn-out vinyl.

They survived as a family mostly because of the little home supplied by Dillon's grandparents. His grandfather was a bricklayer who spent his so-called free time tending a small vineyard. His grandmother worked as head cleaner at one of the beachfront motels. The week Dillon turned eleven, she arranged for him to become the cleaning crew's unofficial helper. She and her husband were both overjoyed when their grandson showed the initiative they had wanted in their own son. Dillon was thrilled beyond words to land a paying job.

Three hours every day, he hauled supplies and soiled linens and freshly washed towels for the cleaning staff. The women flirted outrageously, urging him to grow up faster. Dillon earned fifty cents an hour. He saved every penny. At eleven years of age, he had already taken aim at the exit.

His reverie was broken when the steel door creaked open and Porter announced, "Look who the storm dragged in."

Dillon took his time. Steeling himself the best he could. Ramming the mop home, leaning on it for support. Meeting her gaze because there was nowhere to hide.

Porter actually appeared to be enjoying himself, in a world-weary sort of way. "I believe you two know each other."

3

They exchanged awkward greetings, then stood in the silence of time and everything unsaid. All Olivia could think was, *Eight, nine years gone, and he's as handsome as ever.*

Then a woman called from the station's front office. Dillon excused himself and started down the central corridor, saying, "The supplies we've been waiting for have finally arrived."

Olivia was beyond tired. She wanted a bath and a bed with the shades drawn against the world. Instead, she followed Dillon into the front room. He took an armload of towels and sheets and started back, avoiding her eye as he passed. The gray-haired woman seated behind the main reception desk said, "You're Olivia Greer."

She was tempted to say, *That was long ago.* "Yes."

"Maud Klein. I thought the world of your mother." She possessed the matter-of-fact strength of an experienced officer. "There's a shower room over to your left."

Olivia heard herself say, "I want to help."

"We could sure use it." Maud pointed to a basket resting atop an empty desk. "Carry those donated toys back and instruct the kids to take just one."

She did as Maud instructed, while most of her attention remained on Dillon. He moved with deceptive ease and swiftness, setting out fresh linens in each cell, then returning to strip the mattresses and make a professional job of fitting on new sheets. All the while, he talked softly, flirting with the children. Offering a semblance of hope in a dark time. Drawing smiles from one family after another. Olivia had never met a man who loved work more.

Olivia had spent years surrounded by some of the best-looking people on the planet. Dillon met their measure, and more. His bloodline was California mongrel, a heritage rich in strength and solidity and good nature. She wondered if any of the mothers returning his smile were tempted to neaten his unkempt dark locks. If so, Dillon gave no sign he noticed. His smile, she saw, still held that magnetic glint.

Old memories flooded back. So many good times. Happy, glorious moments.

Discovering what real love tasted like.

Bitter regret. Tear-streaked nights.

Then she stepped into the next cell, and froze.

The cage's occupants were a family of five. The metal bunks were fastened to the side walls, making room for the two mattresses laid out together on the floor. The husband lay on top of an Indian blanket, face tight with pain. His wife saw Olivia's concern and said softly, "Migraine. We're waiting for the medicine to kick in."

"Any minute now," the man murmured.

Her husband was a handsome thirty-something with work-stained hands. His wife was beautiful despite everything. Her features held a balancing act of fatigue and love. She sat with one thigh touching the top of her husband's head, her back propped against the concrete wall. A boy of ten or eleven leaned on her right side, reading from a book they both held.

"*Call of the Wild*," the woman said. "Jack claims it relaxes him. Don't ask me how."

"Read now, talk later," Jack muttered.

Two dark-haired girls aged four or five, obviously twins, nestled like kittens between their father and the wall. One stroked his neck, the other held his hand. One solemnly explained, "We're helping."

"So much," he said softly.

Olivia backed out of the cell and said, "I'll be right back."

She carried the crate back into the office and set it on the desk. Maud asked, "All done?"

"Not yet. Soon." Olivia was filled with an electric

fire so strong it defied her exhaustion. She pushed through the glass doors and rushed across the lot to her car.

She did not realize Dillon had followed her until she heard him say, "Can I have a moment?"

"No time!" She was too busy fumbling with her keys. If anything, the excitement was stronger now. She finally got the trunk open and started pulling at cases.

"Olivia?"

"You can help." She flapped open two silver-coated reflectors. "Take these." She went back to flipping open cases. Canon body. Standard fifty-mil lens. She didn't want to use the flash, but it might be necessary. So that went into her pocket. Slam the trunk. "Hurry!"

She ran.

Across the lot. Through the doors and down the office aisle. Past the officers who gaped at her passage. The flash's cord dangled from her pocket and rattled nervously on the floor. As she started down the jail's corridor, she heard Maud ask, "Porter, what is she doing?"

Thankfully, the family had not moved.

Olivia entered the cell, set down her camera, and knelt by the twins. She had always found it best to address the youngest member of any portrait. The parents would listen, and the young ones tended to do what she wanted if she treated them as important. Which they were. Vital.

She told the girls, "I'd like to take your picture."

The mother asked, "Here? In this place?"

"Right here, right now." Olivia continued to address the wide-eyed girls. "And I'm going to show the world just how beautiful you truly are."

The man started to shift, then stilled when Olivia lifted a single finger.

She waited until he had settled, then went on. "If I can capture this moment, I'm giving it to your family. A Christmas present. Would you like that?"

The twins did what Olivia hoped, which was to look at their mother. When the woman nodded, Olivia rose to her feet. "Here we go."

4

Olivia had left LA with her four favorite cameras and little else besides regret—the Canon and Nikon digitals, Leica for standard film, and a massive antique Graflex that required photographic plates and was an absolute bear to haul around. But under certain conditions the Graflex resulted in breathtaking shots. Not to mention how it remained as precious to Olivia as a childhood teddy.

Olivia knew what had captured Dillon's attention back at the car. The trunk also held stands, lights, and a complete portable sound setup.

As in, no clothes. Or makeup. All that stuff was jammed into a pair of canvas satchels dumped on her rear seat.

No question which to use today. The Canon digital possessed by far the finest array of software for lightning-fast prepping.

Olivia positioned Dillon in the corner opposite the narrow barred window. "Make a semaphore with the reflectors," she told him. "Like you're directing a jet toward the runway. Right arm up, left down. No, Dillon. Your other right." That brought a giggle from the kids. "Good. Now angle the top ten degrees left. Yes. That is your left. Now lift your lower wrist just a smidgen." She used the camera's viewfinder, making sure the barred window now formed a pattern on the wall just overhead. "Outstanding."

Olivia settled into position, a couple of steps closer to the family than Dillon. She addressed the twin not holding her father's hand. "Sweetheart, can you bring your bunny around from your side and set it in your lap?"

She did as requested. "His name is Turtle."

"Okay, that's one for the books. Dillon, the upper reflector, shift a smidgen further right. Half an inch more. Stop. Great, great, great."

The boy asked, "Are you a professional photographer?"

"Pictures now, questions after, okay? Jack, can you please settle back and close your eyes again?"

"A pleasure. Literally."

To the son, "Why don't you go on reading to your dad. Everyone else, please just ignore me. Focus on the story and your father. Pretend I'm magical and am now going to vanish. One, two, three, poof. I'm gone."

It took a few minutes. Not long. The setting was a burden they all carried, a weight so potent they were drawn back in together. She took preliminary photos only because it gradually became just part of the background. Within a couple of minutes, they were a family again.

She whispered, "Perfect."

5

When the photo session ended, Dillon followed Olivia back through the station and into the damp wind. Holding the reflectors had granted him an excuse to study her openly. She was the same beautiful woman he had fallen desperately in love with, yet very different. Same dark blond hair, same balanced features, crystal grey eyes, long pianist's fingers. He wondered if others could see beyond the stain of exhaustion and whatever heartache that had brought her back, and view the lady's resilient strength. The goodness that had always defined her. Everything that made Olivia so special, then and now.

Olivia popped her trunk, then took his reflectors and refolded them with practiced ease. She unlatched the lens, set it in the padded holder, ditto for the camera body. She shut the camera case, pulled her laptop from a nylon satchel, slammed the trunk, plinked the locks, and headed out. Not running. But close.

Olivia did not invite him along, of course. That would have been asking too much. But at least she didn't dismiss him with a polite brush-off.

They were just passing Castaways when she murmured something. Dillon asked, "Did you say something?"

"I wonder if it's still there."

He remained a half step behind her, partly because the sidewalk was too crowded to walk comfortably side by side. But mostly it was so he could observe her. Olivia's impatient haste took him straight back. She was different in so many ways than the woman whose heart he had broken. He glanced down and felt foolish pleasure at the absence of a ring. As he hurried to keep up, he recalled some of their good times. And there had been so many.

Back in their day, Olivia had this way she'd become when something captured her attention. Lady on a mission, was how he'd put it. Totally caught up in the task or quest or whatever. Times like this, her effervescent energy touched everyone within reach. Even now, when the grim weather was reflected in most faces. Dillon wondered if she was even aware of how many people stopped and stared. Or if she even realized when it started raining.

"At least the store's still here." Olivia pushed open the glass door, and smiled at the old-fashioned bell that pinged its welcome. "Hi, Mr. Gleason!"

The African-American was too tall to be considered fat. More like a well-fleshed, big-boned, aging boxer. Big everything—hands, head, body, frown. "Who's this, now?"

"You know perfectly well."

"My stars and stripes, Olivia Greer, is that really you?"

"Nobody says that anymore. Stars and stripes." She crossed the shop and set her laptop on the counter. "It sounds vaguely profane."

"Well, I'll certainly come to you when I'm concerned about profanity." He squinted at Dillon, declared, "Well, I never."

"Hi, Mr. Gleason."

"It never ceases to amaze, what this storm keeps dragging in." His gaze went back to where Olivia took a flash drive from her pocket and fit it into a holder shaped as a USB memory stick. But Dillon suspected the man continued to address him. "You of all people I'd have thought would have more sense."

Dillon shrugged. "Nowhere else to go."

Olivia cast Dillon a glance. One open enough for him to glimpse inside the shadow caves encircling her gaze.

Then Olivia went back to working her mousepad. "What's the largest size high-quality paper you've got in stock?"

"So good to see you looking so well, Mr. Gleason. After all this time, you're as handsome as ever."

Olivia looked up. "Print first, dance later. That okay with you?"

"Do I have a choice?"

She went back to her laptop. "No."

He moved smoothly for such a big man. Two minutes later he returned and said, "We're out of A0. Haven't had a delivery in weeks. Sixteen sheets left of A1."

She leaned in closer to the screen. "Quality?"

Gleason tsked. "You know me better than that."

She glanced up again and did her best to smile. "Sorry."

"You want glossy, matte, or raw cotton blend?"

"I'm working in black and white."

"Glossy it is."

"Do you have frames? Passe-partouts?"

"Different question, same answer."

Dillon cleared his throat and asked her, "Can you tell me what you're doing?"

Somewhere along the line, Olivia had learned how to talk while still working at hyper-speed. "The debate over lenses, digital bodies, and software is endless. I've read and studied most of the sites that don't descend into verbal violence and scathing put-downs."

He had no idea what she was talking about, and really didn't care. "Okay, so?"

"I personally think there's a great deal of truth and value to all sides of the equation. For my money, the Nikon system is tops when it comes to deep-color saturation and finesse. But it also requires a huge amount of time to get right. The choices are basically endless. I love working with my buddy Nikon when time is not a factor."

"So, not today."

"Definitely not. When it comes to auto-tuning and fast turnaround, setting a preliminary standard and trusting the system to make it pop, for my money it's Canon hands down." She leaned down so close her nose almost touched the screen. Shifted back and worked the mousepad with one hand, the keyboard with her other. "The Nikon pros treat me like a second-class shooter. Barely above amateur status. Needing the computer and the camera to do most of the work." She inspected again, nodded, and slapped the computer shut. Pulled out the SSD and holder. Offered it to Gleason. "You know where they can stick it, right?"

He accepted the stick. "Whatever you say."

"The one I'm after is labeled A1."

Gleason waggled his finger back and forth between them. "Are you two . . ."

"No," Dillon said.

Olivia snapped, "Can we please dispense with the ridiculous and get to work here?"

* * *

Soon as Gleason retreated to the back room, the shop was filled with an awkward tension. All the unspoken thoughts and memories, all the regrets, all the arguments they never finished. He had no idea what to say. Or even if it would be better for them both if he just left. So there he stood, midway between the counter and the exit, watching her trace one finger over the laptop's corner.

Then she said, "After everything fell apart, I kept thinking if I could just hold on to the one thing I had left, it might turn out okay. Someday."

Her voice was calm, almost matter-of-fact. Dillon's only response was to take a step to his right, so he could see her face more clearly.

Olivia seemed to approve of his silence. Or maybe she wasn't speaking to him at all. She wrapped her arms around her middle and gazed at the counter. "When I saw that family in the jail cell, it all came together. Just for a second. There and gone in the space of two breaths. But right then, it felt . . ."

"Tell me. Please."

"I thought maybe this was it. A step in the right direction. Using my gift, trying to help . . ."

Gleason reentered the shop.

He held an oversized photo sheet in both hands. The big man approached the counter slowly, his expression solemn, his movements almost theatrical. He used two fingers to shift Olivia's laptop over. Then he settled the sheet on the counter. Swung it around so it faced her. Took a step back.

Olivia just stood there. Dillon could not see if she even breathed. "Can I see?" When neither Olivia or the big man responded, he stepped forward.

The picture *arrested* him.

Gleason said, "If they ever do a picture book of this Christmas season in Miramar . . ." He used two fingers to shift the print ever so slightly. "I want this on the cover."

Olivia remained frozen. Unblinking.

"I don't know how. But you've captured what a lot of us are feeling. How we're there for them." He tapped the print's corner. "These people. We care and we do what we can."

The resolution was crystal sharp. The work held an ethereal quality, too precise to be a painting, and yet that was how it seemed. This was more than just another portrait. The family *spoke* to him.

The light was dim enough to soften their weary state. They were transformed into a mystical tableau.

The wall behind the family was splashed with the window's gray illumination. The bars formed a cross-hatch pattern above the five people. The love they shared, despite everything, made Dillon want to shout out loud.

Instead, all he could manage was, "Olivia. Wow."

Gleason said, "I work with photographers and editors serving regional magazines and papers. Santa Barbara to San Jose. Everybody's looking for something that speaks to the season. Not happy. But, you know . . ."

"Beautiful," Dillon said. "Despite everything."

"There you go." Gleason made another minute adjustment to the print's angle. "Okay if I share this around?"

Olivia did not respond.

Gleason lifted his gaze. Studied the silent woman on the counter's other side. "Had to be something pretty awful, bringing you back here now. Despite all the reasons to stay away."

Olivia did not move, much less speak.

He tapped the print a third time. "The young lady who left here with dreams too big for Miramar to hold, she's come back an artist, sure enough."

Dillon saw a single tear escape and trickle down her cheek. It came as close as anything in his own hard season to breaking his heart.

Gleason said, "I'm not sure I believed the legend of the phoenix before now."

They remained like that, held by the momentary amber. Despite everything.

Olivia sniffed, then said, "Can I please have one more on the raw cotton stock?"

"Thought you'd say that." Gleason lifted the print

from the counter. "Come back and help me frame this while I run off the print. And an additional one for me, okay?"

"If you want."

"Lady, this is going in my front window." To Dillon, "Step around the counter, will you? Mind the shop. Come on, darling. Let's get to work."

6

A rising wind off the Pacific threatened to turn their framed prints into sails. Dillon kept a tight grip on the protective Bubble Wrap and held the frame sideways to the blow. At least the rain had momentarily paused.

They hurried back up the six blocks, stepping into the road where the sidewalks became clogged with people going nowhere. Tangled remnants of Christmas decorations still clung to streetlights and overhead cables, spinning frantically in the rising wind. The air tasted damp. The clouds swirled and churned.

Despite everything, Dillon was as happy as he'd been in a long time. In a way, it made little sense. Nothing about his own state had changed. Just the same, he was back in the company of his first true love. They were doing something together, sharing an act that had made a deep impression on them both. For the moment, it was enough.

They slipped through the fence surrounding the station lot. The main entrance faced inland, so that the building blocked much of the wind. Olivia unlocked her car and slipped the print she carried into the rear seat. She then joined Dillon under the broad overhang, sheltered from rain now spackling the cars. She spoke in a voice scarcely audible over the strengthening storm. "You broke my heart."

It was an accusation nine years in the making. Dillon was almost glad to have it out in the open. "I've written you a hundred apologies. Late at night. In my head. And heart. I just never had the courage to actually put pen to paper." He lowered the print so that it balanced on his right shoe. "Plus you'd gotten married and moved to LA. I wasn't sure you actually wanted to hear from me."

"I didn't, truth be told. Not for the longest while."

"For what it's worth, I'm sorry. Truly, deeply sorry. I should have handled it better. Been straight with you about . . ."

"Everything."

He nodded. "Especially the timing. My big chance came, and we'd just broken up again, and so I left."

"You ran away."

He wanted to argue, just like before. She'd always had the ability to press his red button. Ever since they were kids, Olivia could send him into full-rage mode with a single word, sometimes just a look. The way she'd responded, just as furious and sometimes more so, had left him helpless.

But they weren't kids anymore. And the arguments never got them anywhere. "I didn't run from you."

"Oh, really."

"No. I ran from our arguments. From how we never could hold on to peace, not for more than a night."

"And then you got your big chance."

"I did."

"Which you never told me about."

"No." Big breath. "And I should have. Even though I knew it would be the worst argument of all. Me going. Without you. So yeah. I ran away. But mostly I was running from here. This place. It was as tight a cage as the cells back inside there."

She was quiet now. Thoughtful. "I felt that too."

"I know you did." He took a huge risk, reached out, settled his hand on her shoulder. "I'm so sorry, Olivia. I was desperate, I was angry, I was hurting, and none of that is any excuse. I should have done things better."

She examined his face, her expression thoughtful. "Gleason was right. We were just another pair of lonely kids with dreams too big for Miramar." She flinched as the wind blew rain under the awning. "Let's get inside."

*   *   *

Olivia knew Dillon thought they had stopped under the awning so she could speak of past deeds and broken hearts. But in truth that almost came out unbidden. She had been thinking of their ending, of course. Not the last time they were together. She couldn't remember that at all. Some argument. One of many. Shouting with the furious abandon of kids who did not know how to hold back. And that's what they were, of course. Two very young people who knew nothing of the world beyond Miramar, who were so intent on breaking out they fought against everything and everyone. Especially those closest to them. The people with whom they should have been gentle. And almost never were.

All that was with her still as she entered the station. But none of it was why she had stopped beneath the rain-swept awning.

Despite the storm and the empty season and how tonight she would share a jail cell with strangers, Olivia had been struck by the most astonishing of thoughts. Standing there in the gray dusk, Dillon holding the framed print and following her lead, she had found herself turning away from everything that had brought her to this moment.

For that one brief instant, Olivia found herself looking toward an unseen tomorrow.

It was such a sudden and unexpected experience, she became welded to the spot. Wondering what on earth it might mean. If there truly was something, anything . . .

Porter stood by Maud's desk, his hands filled with papers. He glanced up and told Dillon, "We could use some help, shifting mattresses and linens into our new bachelors' pad."

"No problem." He asked Olivia, "Can I show them?"

She moved toward the side wall, so as to observe him and the print and the officers. Dillon showed the same eager pride she had known and loved, all those many eons ago.

Dillon remained where he was, scarcely two steps inside the doorway. "Olivia, please."

"Go ahead."

Dillon mimicked Gleason's slow and formal movements. He set the frame on an empty desk and kept the print facing away from the officers as he freed it from the packing. When he turned it around, he offered a quiet, "Ta-dah."

Porter, Maud, and the detective whose name Olivia couldn't remember, they all moved together. Bouncing off unseen barriers. Drawn to the image.

Maud said, "Oh my sweet word."

Porter said, "Olivia, this is . . ."

Dillon shifted slightly to one side, his head turning from the print to the officers to Olivia and back again. "I know, right?"

Then Olivia remembered the detective's name. Ryan. Ryan Eames said, "Police officers aren't allowed to cry while on duty. It's in the rule book. I'm sure of it."

Porter said, "My two ladies have got to see this."

Olivia loved being able to observe Dillon. His pride and sheer unabashed joy defied the gray afternoon. He had always been her number-one cheerleader. Until that awful day when he was gone.

She heard herself say, "I have a second print in the car. I wanted to take it home, you know, whenever. You're welcome to borrow it."

It was Maud who said, "This is staying right here. With us."

The chief protested, "Maud . . ."

"Porter, those ladies of yours can come in and look at it anytime they want." To Olivia, "Thank you, dear. This will brighten up our season."

"You're welcome." Olivia walked over and took the frame from Dillon. When she started toward the cells, she discovered all the others followed.

The husband was seated up now, color back in his face. But there was still an air of fragility surrounding the strong man. The wife and son shared the mattress with him, the boy still reading as she appeared in the doorway. One of the twins was snuggled in his lap, the other leaned against his side while still holding the oddly named rabbit.

Olivia walked over, knelt before the mattress, and set the frame down in front of her.

The wife gasped. Or sobbed. Or both.

Once again Olivia addressed the twins. "When I came here, I was very sad. Doing this for you makes me feel like I have a reason to hope."

The twin holding Turtle said, "That's what Mommy says about me."

Her mother corrected, "About both of you."

Olivia loved having a reason to smile. From the heart. Holding nothing back. "Merry Christmas."

Olivia woke sometime after midnight, and discovered she shared her pallet with one of the twins. She lay feeling the girl's warmth cuddled to her side, when soft voices drifted in from the station. She was drawn to full wakefulness by the sound of Dillon's laugh.

As she rose, the little girl whimpered but did not fully waken. Olivia left the cell she shared with the family and followed the voices into the front room.

Dillon and the dark-haired police detective were seated by the front desk. Dillon rose to his feet and said in greeting, "There's overcooked coffee and ginseng tea."

"Tea. Definitely."

"And honey."

"You're singing my midnight melody."

"I'll get it." He indicated the woman still seated be-hind the desk. "You remember Ryan."

Olivia sketched a wave. "I was sure we had met, but I couldn't remember when."

"Lucky you," Dillon said. "Ryan arrested my pop."

"My first bust after joining the Miramar force," Ryan said. She had a cop's smile, tight and sharpened by many hard nights. Just the same, there was a warmth to her. A depth. "Then Porter said we should let it go with a warning."

Dillon emerged with a steaming mug. "Porter is a wise man. And a good cop."

"Now that is something I can agree with," Ryan said. "How did you turn out like you did?"

"My grandparents helped," Dillon replied. "Mostly I was too busy breaking free to pay my folks any at-tention." He handed Olivia her mug, then asked the detective, "Can I freshen that for you?"

"Tea sounds great. Only don't use all of Maud's honey. She'll skin us both." Ryan turned her attention to Olivia. "That picture you made of the family was really, really beautiful."

"Thank you."

Ryan watched him pull up a third chair, waited for Olivia to settle, then said, "Dillon tells me you left Miramar for LA."

"Eight and a half years ago."

"You worked as a professional photographer?"

Olivia waited as Dillon shifted closer and directed her answers at him. Not looking his way. There was no need. "I mostly worked on movie sets."

"Making films?"

"No. That is the cinematographer's job. A totally different field. I was contracted by a studio's PR department. I shot supposedly casual photographs. Which were almost always totally staged. Pictures that could be shared with bloggers and the entertainment channels. Sometimes I shot taped interviews. But mostly I did stills." They were both silent, which allowed her to drift back. Drawn by their interest and the midnight hour. Back to the good days. "Nowadays the big stars almost always demand a closed set. Meaning no outside interviewer or photographer can enter. They gradually came to trust me. I only gave out shots that put them at their best light. Then some of the older stars asked me to do some promo stills. Photos they could keep on hand for whatever. They liked the way I shaped the image."

"I believe it," Dillon said.

Ryan asked, "What happened?"

"The sky fell."

Ryan looked out the front doors, to where rain had turned silver by the station lights. "There's a lot of that going around."

"Tell me about it," Dillon agreed.

Ryan said, "I've recently remarried. Come the new year, my husband is formally adopting my son by a previous marriage. I'd love to have a portrait of us." When Olivia did not reply, she added, "I can pay."

"I could certainly use the income." Olivia sipped from her mug. "For years I've wanted to become a portrait photographer. But the competition in LA is so fierce, and the ranks are basically closed. Work like that goes to the big names."

Dillon was smiling now. "And look what's happened."

Ryan asked, "Is that a yes?"

7

The next morning, Dillon woke to the sound of children's laughter. The sound was so unexpected, he thought perhaps it was part of some dream he had carried from sleep. Then a child sang a few notes, followed by more laughter. It filled the empty back cell where Dillon lay, clear as the California sunlight he suspected he would not see that day.

He lay there, alone in the station's drunk tank. The floor canted ever so slightly toward a drain in the room's center. Dillon had set his mattress so his feet were by the drain and his head by the metal shelf running along the back wall. It was a very odd place to feel as complete as he did now. Perhaps it was simply because he had slept well for the first time since leaving his former home in Philadelphia. Yet as he lay there, staring at the concrete ceiling, he recalled the previous day. Helping Olivia find her way to some semblance of a new beginning. He had no idea what

had drawn her back to Miramar in such an unwel-
coming season. But there in the shadows she carried,
he had sensed a similar tale to his own.

Watching Olivia photograph the family and prepare the portrait had carried seeds of hope. Fragile
and tiny. But there just the same.

Dillon lay on his back, fingers laced behind his
head, and allowed his mind to roam. Something he
rarely did. His previous existence had been too full,
too fast, too focused on everything that filled his
days. All that was gone now. It was far from pleasant,
looking back. Just the same, it felt right. Lying here in
his solitary cell, remembering.

Soon after Dillon turned eleven, his hippie mom
left his hippie dad. One day she was there, and their
homelife was okay. Not great. More like, what
passed for normal. Then one night she had declared
that she was so bored with her existence it felt like
her soul had entered hibernation. Three days later,
she was gone.

His father's response was to lose himself in smoke.
Weed intake went up tenfold. Dillon's old man checked
out so far and so fast he could go days without even
speaking. His only remaining interest was tending his
crop of weed. Certainly not his son.

Dillon's grandparents had insisted he live with his
father and effectively babysit the stoned loner. But
they sheltered their grandson in so many ways. Every

few evenings he joined them for dinner. His grandmother then sent Dillon home with food to tide them
over. His grandparents started treating him as a newly
forged adult. One they could trust to keep things together, both for himself and his childish dad. Later
that year his grandmother arranged Dillon's unofficial job at the motel. Dillon discovered a genuine passion for work, and doing a job well.

The jail's regular showers and facilities had been
sealed off. Instead, the station's new guests used the
bathroom next to the chief's office. Two handmade
signs hung to either side of the door. The first was a
circle with an arrow that swiveled, pointing to either
MALE or FEMALE. The second sign simply said, BE-
HAVE.

Dillon showered and dressed in wrinkled but clean
clothes, then followed his nose toward coffee and
breakfast. Two officers served duty by the front reception desk. Chief Porter leaned over Maud's shoulder and studied a file, while she quietly pointed her
way down the page.

The six families who had spent the night in the
cells were clustered around a pair of desks adjacent to
the kitchenette. Older kids played a board game
while the twins stood to either side of Olivia's chair,
wearing police hats and clutching stuffed animals and
vying for her attention. Olivia's family portrait now
hung on the wall behind them.

Dillon accepted a plate of overcooked eggs and ate staring out the front window. The rain had stopped, but the sky remained a leaden gray. He returned his empty plate to the kitchenette, refilled his mug, and headed over. Olivia told him, "The twins think they're leaving today."

The girl with the misnamed bunny announced, "Mommy says tomorrow. Daddy says now."

Olivia went on, "Porter says the dozers have been out this morning. The roads to our homes have been cleared. He can't say for how long. The hillsides are just waiting for an excuse to send down more rubble."

"Which is what Daddy told Mommy," the twin reported. "Six times."

Dillon said, "We could drive up together, if you like. Me and you. Just take a look. Not even go inside unless . . ."

"That's why I've been sitting here," she replied. "Hoping you'd say that."

Dillon had a rental car that might get them there and back. Ditto for Olivia's Honda. But just as likely either vehicle would leave them stranded somewhere that turned awful when the rains resumed. He walked to where Porter continued frowning over a form Maud held and asked, "Can I have a word?"

"Anything to get me away from this mess."

Maud said, "Our chief suffers from a severe case of formaphobia."

Porter turned his back to the room, lowered his voice, and said, "I was hoping Olivia would do pictures of my family. Our daughter's grown up. This may be her last Christmas at home."

Maud rose and planted herself alongside Porter. Her voice was scarcely above a whisper. "I'd love one of the grandkids."

"We can pay," Porter said.

"We see the state she's in," Maud said. "We were wondering what you thought of the idea."

"I imagine Olivia will agree," Dillon said. "But first we need to borrow somebody's four-wheel drive."

There were worse ways to travel inland, Dillon thought, than in the chief's own pickup. Town shields on the doors, lights and sirens discreetly tucked away but there in an emergency, three antennas and a radio that could probably reach Mars, massive lights on the roof, four-wheel drive, six-liter diesel kicker. All the comforts of home.

The rain had stopped, but the sky remained a dismal gray. Olivia rode curled in the manner of a teen, shoes kicked off, seatbelt loose around her middle, heels propped on the seat, arms wrapped around her legs. They did not speak for a time, taking the main road leading east. Past the grocery store and the new strip mall beyond, into the largest of Miramar valleys. Like so many drives before, back in the bygone days when all they could think of was how to escape.

He knew her so well. The looks she cast. The questions she didn't ask, because she didn't want to pressure him into speaking about what hurt. Which it did. Even staying silent burned his throat and heart. So he decided he might as well get it over with.

He started with a statement. "You know about Wharton."

She straightened in her seat. The ease gone now. It no longer suited what was happening. "Of course I know."

Dillon had skipped his junior year, which meant they graduated high school together. They had both won partial scholarships to UC Santa Cruz, close enough they could commute for the first two years. Then Olivia's photography began winning prizes, and UC Santa Barbara's art department reached out, offering a full ride. UCSB's art school was considered a gateway to greatness. Of course she went, and their relationship became defined by weekends in Miramar. Olivia racing toward her exit, Dillon plodding stolidly along. Until Wharton.

"After you left for Santa Barbara, I started working on a double major," he told her. "Econ and accounting. Honors in both."

"Why am I only hearing about this now?"

"Don't give me that. You know perfectly well why."

She leaned her head back against the headrest. Sighed. "I know."

Their weekends reached a fever pitch, the good times flaming with a unique brilliance, the bad times wreaking havoc and destruction. Olivia's mother had repeatedly warned they were playing with fire, hurting along with them, fearful for how they both seemed almost eager to find the exit.

Which, truth be told, was how Dillon had seen it all too often. Driving back to Santa Cruz, molten with fury over whatever slight he felt able to carry away from their latest quarrel. Severing one cord after another. Letting go.

Olivia brought him back with, "Wharton."

"It was everything I'd hoped for and more," he said, remembering. "I didn't know how lucky I was until I got there. My accounting prof had urged me to apply, and she was totally right. There was none of the snobbishness, none of the country-club attitude that defined other top-tier business schools. Wharton brought in a lot of kids like me. We competed, we fought, we learned."

She said quietly, "You found a home. At long last."

Being understood should not have hurt like it did. "Four months before graduation, I was recruited. The thrill of having several groups compete for me

was something I can't describe. I went with a bou-
tique investment fund, they specialized in high-tech
start-ups. Solid returns." He went quiet. Remembering.

"Problems?"

"I assumed Wharton's level playing field would
exist in the real world. I was wrong. I lost out to
Yalies on promotions I deserved. Twice. The third
time, I left. I started an investment advisory group
with five others from our group who also suffered
from this unlevel playing field. Our former employers
accused us of stealing clients. Which was true and not
true. The clients didn't withdraw anything, they simply gave their next tranche of funds to us. Our former
group threatened us with a court action, then they
went silent." A pause, then, "I thought we were in the
clear."

The valley narrowed. The road went down to one
lane, the other blocked by piles of rubble. They
passed scrapers gathering piles and pouring them into
gravel trucks. The noise was fierce. Going was slow
enough for Dillon to become mired in memories.

When they were past and the going quieter, Olivia
pressed, "What happened?"

"I thought I had discovered a major new investment opportunity. It seemed almost too perfect. Which,
it turned out, is exactly what it was."

"They set you up." She reached across the divide
and settled her hand on his shoulder. "I'm so sorry."

Her hand threatened to brand him. "We went all in. Urged our investors to do the same. They trusted us. I lost everything."

They reached the narrow road leading up to their homes. Piles of rocks and debris rose like prehistoric grave mounds to either side. The latest storms had loosened more rubble. Dillon moved forward at a crawl. Tempted to go quiet. Pretend it was over. But he knew it wouldn't work. If he didn't finish the telling, the unspoken final chapter would keep burning. "Top investment funds form a pretty tight niche. My former company spread rumors that I didn't just fail my investors. I stole funds. Making sure I could never go back. Three and a half weeks ago, I gave up. Declared bankruptcy. Selling everything and wrapping up my former life took until this week."

There was really nothing to be said after that.

Dillon pushed the four-wheel drive over gravel and loose boulders, climbing steadily. All the while, Olivia remained curled in her seat, facing him, holding his shoulder, saying sorry in her own uniquely silent manner. Just like the very best of their former days.

When they reached her drive, Dillon asked, "Ready?"

She slipped her hand back, swung around, straightened in her seat. "Absolutely not."

He pressed on the gas. "Here we go."

*   *   *

Dillon pulled through the sycamores that flanked the entrance and stopped. When Olivia did not move, he said, "Let me do this."

Olivia remained silent.

He went on, "There's no need for you to go in. Not today. I'll check things out, make sure it's as safe as it can be. We'll head back to town. Leave this place in our rearview mirror."

Olivia responded by reaching for her purse. She handed over a set of keys and said, "Thank you, Dillon."

He carefully tread through the muddy terrain. The cottage stood on a tiny knob, and the flow of mud and debris had flowed along a shallow defile on the hill's opposite side.

Throughout his childhood, farms and hillside homes had gradually been bought up by wealthy outsiders and turned into weekend retreats, retirement homes, investment properties. His and Olivia's families were holdouts.

The hilltop formed a trio of descending levels. His father's ratty home and marijuana garden occupied the next property, while his grandparents' home and vineyard crowned the gentle slope. The storms had carved a muddy furrow farther north. From where he stood, Dillon could see how old-growth trees and the vineyard's retaining walls had acted like a dam, mostly protecting the three homes. But a minor segment of the mudslide had crossed behind Olivia's cottage, shoving it partly off the foundations.

He climbed the front porch and took a moment to examine the home's exterior. It looked to be fairly intact, but weathered by seven years of renters. He unlocked the front door, then used both hands and some very hard effort to pull it open.

The home was a weary shell. The power was off, and water from a burst pipe had stained the living room carpet. The hardwood floors were scarred and dirty. Dillon forced himself forward, hurting for the lady waiting in the pickup.

He swiftly made his way through the two bedrooms, the baths, the hall, the indentation where the dining table once stood. Most of the walls were riven by new cracks, some so large he could see daylight. The kitchen floor had crimped up, sealing the door leading to the rear veranda.

Dillon confronted memories everywhere. Olivia's mother did not so much raise wildflowers as invite them to grow. She bundled them, selecting as much for fragrance as colors, and hung them around the veranda's high beams. Out where the river of mud had erased the rear garden, she had raised vegetables and kept two dozen hives, producing honey she sold in town. There had been money from somewhere; Olivia's mother never spoke about the life or family she had left long ago. The only family Dillon ever met was Olivia's aunt, a big-boned woman whose size had astonished him. She had a laugh so huge a younger Dillon had wondered if maybe someday she might boom so loudly she would blow out the windows.

He walked back through the kitchen and the parlor. Stepped onto the front porch. Shoved hard on the door, jamming it shut. Pocketed the key. Started down the front steps. Crossed the yard. Olivia watched in silence as he opened the driver's door, slid inside, and started the motor.

Dillon took it easy turning around, carefully forging a path through the slick debris. Beyond the front gates he turned right and gunned the engine, pushing the truck up the incline. Toward home.

Now that they had left her cottage in the rearview mirror, Olivia released a long breath and asked, "How bad was it?"

"I'm no expert. But it wasn't good."

Another breath, then, "I can't live there, can I."

"Not without a lot of work."

"Which I can't afford."

Dillon had no idea how to respond, and remained silent.

The entry to the home where Dillon had grown up was blocked by debris. But their view from the road showed him all he needed to see. The debris-flow had come closer to the house and the damage was more severe. Much of the garden was gone. One corner of the home's foundations had been eaten away, so that the house tilted at a severe angle. A single breath, a finger's touch, and it would join the muddy descent. From inside the truck he could see loose foundations, the cracked walls, the shattered glass.

Olivia said, "I'm sorry, Dillon."

He drove on. "Don't be. It was never much of a home."

"How often did you come back?"

"A couple of times each year, never for very long. Then my grandparents passed away two years ago. There wasn't much reason after that. You?"

"Not since I married Gavin. Mom moved to Phoenix and lived with my aunt. She claimed it was too lonely up here without me. She rented out the cottage and lived from the proceeds. The cancer took her three years ago." A trace of a smile. "To say she and Gavin didn't get along is the understatement of the century."

"So she never visited you in LA?"

"Once. After I miscarried."

"I'm so sorry, Olivia. I didn't know."

"No way you could have." A silence, then, "I'm glad Mom isn't around to see what's happened."

Dillon nodded. "She loved that old place, sure enough."

As Dillon turned off the road and climbed the graveled track, he remembered running back and forth between the homes, taking trails through stands of California sycamore, arroyo willow, bay laurel, and oak. He was glad to see most of the trees had survived the storms, anchoring the property. He rounded the final bend, stopped the truck, and squinted through the rain-streaked windshield.

Dillon's grandfather had been passionate about everything that grew on his land. The otherwise silent man sounded almost lyrical when he talked about his trees, his garden, his vines. The gentle slopes pointing west and south had held almost four acres of vineyards, producing what locals had claimed was the worst wine in all California.

Olivia said, "It looks okay."

He nodded agreement. In truth, he thought the home looked more or less intact. This high up, the mud flow had not been so powerful, and the glade of old trees had firmly anchored the home and barn. Even the low wall surrounding his grandmother's vegetable garden looked intact.

Olivia asked, "Do you want me to go inside?"

"Not unless you want to."

"In that case, I'll stay right here."

Dillon made a fast circuit, lingering just long enough to ensure the place was habitable. Once the power and water were back, he had a place to live. If he could manage to endure the memories. And the regret. He returned to the living room, breathing in the cold dusty aroma of his grandfather's pipe. He had fought so hard to leave this place. And look where it had gotten him.

8

It was dark when they finally reached Miramar's outskirts. Traffic was heavy in the other direction, a long stream of headlights heading out while the roads remained open. For Olivia, the return journey held a calmness that defied all the concerns binding them to this place and season.

Much of the town remained blacked out, even the streetlights were off. She saw several power company trucks and workers high up in their cherry-pickers. She had nowhere else to live except the jail. No place where she might stay and recover. These were very real concerns. Just the same, it felt so good to sit with her back against the side door, shoes off, legs up on the seat, chin resting on her knees. Like she had so very many times before. In the era she thought lost and gone forever.

She asked, "You never married?"

"Year before last I got engaged. Great lady. It didn't take." He took it slow around a rubble-strewn curve. "She wanted what I couldn't give her."

"What was that?"

"A husband." He flashed her an almost-smile. "I was working crazy hours, traveling all over the place, sizing up new investments, everything it took to help my tiny little egg of a company hatch and grow wings."

She had a crazy thought, one definitely best left unsaid. How he had suffered through his own version of a miscarriage. She needed to say something, and came up with, "You would have been a great boss."

He pulled up to a small crossroads, the darkened streetlight dangling overhead. He looked at her, started to speak, then something beyond her window caught Dillon's eye. "Get a load of that."

She lowered her feet, turned, and said, "Oh, Dillon."

The single-story ranch was surrounded by Christmas. Only the lights were out, and the front yard's trees danced in the wind. The sleigh and reindeer bounding across the roof were mere shadows. Ditto for the tall candy canes and figurines filling the yard.

Instead, every window held candles.

Dozens of them glowed and flickered in silent defiance of the night.

Olivia reached for his hand.

They sat like that for a long moment, until the car behind them beeped softly. A quick, almost apologetic tap. The sound of another traveler touched by what they saw.

Dillon released her hand and drove on. "Now I remember what it feels like."

"What?"

"Something I thought I'd left behind," he replied. He continued in silence until they pulled into the station lot. Dillon cut the engine, then finished, "Hope."

Dillon entered the station long enough to thank Porter for the loan, then together they walked to the Ocean Avenue Grill. A heavy cloud cover glinted copper from the streetlights still working. To the west, the Pacific rumbled like a coming storm. They entered by the kitchen door, sat on stools behind the larder, and devoured the day's simple fare.

As they finished eating, Dillon told her about Porter wanting a family portrait. And Maud and Ryan asking as well. Olivia found it necessary to swallow hard before replying, "I would like that more than anything."

"Maud and Ryan can definitely wait," Dillon continued. "But Porter's daughter is leaving tomorrow for school."

"Tomorrow is fine." Another hard swallow. "I run away as hard and fast as I can get. I come back, thinking I'm totally defeated. And I'm greeted by a ruined house, a jail cell for a bed, and the first faint glimmer of a dream come true."

Dillon studied her in silence.

"What?"

He shook his head. "I'm happy for you."

Olivia did not press. As they departed, Olivia hugged Claire and pretended to ignore her friend smirking over seeing the two of them together.

On the way back to the station, Olivia said, "Maybe it's time you give me a fuller picture of the cottage."

Dillon's response was calmly apologetic. Not so much offhand as preoccupied. He described the loose foundations, the damaged retaining wall, the stripped kitchen, the broken glass. His casual manner helped her accept the news.

When he finished, she repeated what she had said on the road. "I don't have the funds to put things right."

"Of course money's a factor," he replied. "But at some point you'll need to decide whether you should just start over."

"Different question, same answer." A light rain started, scarcely more than a drifting fog. Even so, the faces she saw along the crowded sidewalk looked worried. And exhausted. She was very glad for Dillon's company. "I don't have anywhere to live."

"Of course you do."

"I'm not talking about the jail. I am very nearly broke. I feel like I've spent the past few months standing by this great swollen river. Watching events I can't control and mostly don't understand sweep away everything I've built."

"You've come back home with a talent, a gift. Something you can build on."

"Home," she repeated softly. "You just said I don't have one."

Dillon stopped, waited for her to face him, and said, "You're moving into my grandparents' home. With me."

"Dillon, thank you. So much. But I don't think that's a good idea."

"Listen to what I'm saying." Firm, solid, definite. "What's past is past. But we're still friends, aren't we?"

"Of course we are."

"The old place has three bedrooms. Two baths. We'll share. You take your time. Try to work out what you want for a next step." He waved toward the unseen hills. "When you start working up your next temper tantrum, we'll flip to see who's sleeping in the barn."

"I don't have tantrums."

"Oh really. Maybe it's just my memory playing tricks."

"Obviously." She used both hands and cleared her face. "You were always there for me."

"Not always." Dillon took a very hard breath. "I'm so sorry, Olivia. I knew I was hurting you, leaving like I did."

"You were angry."

"I was. And desperate to get away. And so many other things. It all got mixed up inside. My grandad gave me his old truck. I piled everything I owned in the back, covered it in a tarp, and set off. Drove sixteen hours that first day. Doing my level best not to look in the rearview mirror. Deliriously happy to finally break free of my old man. And brokenhearted, no matter how often I told myself it was the only way."

She remained silent for a time, then said softly, "Maybe it was. You had to go. I knew that. I wanted it to be LA. And yet . . ."

He whispered, "Tell me."

But it was to herself that she spoke. Confessing the impossible. "I wanted you to come. Desperately. But I fought against it too."

"We both did." His response was barely a whisper. "All the time."

"I wanted to be free. I love you. Loved. So much. But I couldn't see how to have you near and still . . ."

"Become who you are." He nodded. "I see that."

"Did you feel the same?"

"Olivia, maybe. At some level. But you were always the smarter one. The one who saw things first. I was too busy fighting to get away."

She felt as if a great weight had suddenly been lifted. One she had not even known she'd been carrying. "I'm glad we talked. Now let's get out of the rain."

9

When Dillon emerged from his cell that next morning, he discovered all the remaining families were on the move. Only Olivia still slumbered in her pallet. The family with the portrait left a thank-you poster pinned to her blanket. The twins had decorated the page with a lady holding a camera and huge smile. Dillon used the shower, ate another plate of overcooked eggs, wished the families a safe journey, and left the station.

The sky was heavy with swirling gray clouds. There was no wind and the air tasted damp, laden with coming rain. He walked to the café, doctored his coffee, and headed down Ocean Avenue. The sidewalks were almost empty, and those people he passed walked with the sleepy haste of locals on their way to starting another day. Everyone he saw, including those talking on phones and texting, cast worried glances toward the sky.

The light was not so much dim as tainted. Even so, it felt good to be out alone, walking the streets of his childhood. He had been woken that morning by the same image that had carried him to sleep. He could not say precisely why candles in a home's every window would impact him as they did. Lying in his pallet in the windowless cell, Dillon had felt both comforted and unsettled by the memory.

But the dream that had pushed him from sleep and hastened his departure had been something else entirely. In it, he stood in front of that same darkened house. A hard rain fell, pushed in all directions by a blustery wind. But there he stood, untouched by the storm. The window glowed with the light of just one candle, so brilliant it turned the raindrops molten and gold.

Then the dream shifted.

First the window vanished. Then the house. The candle remained there, poised in the dark. The storm blew harder still, but it could not touch either of them. Not the night, not the rain.

When he woke, he had the strongest sense that the candle came with him. Out of his dream, into the jail.

As he continued down Ocean Avenue, he remained filled with the night's conflicting emotions. Comfort and tumult both. A peace and an unsettled urge to rise up and do something.

There was hardly any mystery to that particular desire. His answer to every childhood hardship had been the same. It formed some of his earliest and finest memories. Work had bound him to his silent grandparents and sheltered him from his permanently stoned father. He had been far from the most intelligent student, not in school or university or business school. But he worked with passion. With a genuine sense of satisfaction in getting it right, finding the answer, moving on. The loss of his business and all his future dreams had been made far worse by having no place to go. No new work, nothing to salve the wounds.

Dillon reached the turning onto the oceanfront road, and froze at the sight.

Police tape sealed off the main parking lot. The far edge had crumbled and fallen into the sea. The ocean was still, slick, gray as the sky. Pilings and trees floated in the quiet waters. The ocean walk was shattered in places. The tall pillars meant to hold the connecting bridge-walks dangled empty and forlorn.

Then he saw the people.

Dozens of locals walked the beach and road both, hefting timber and carrying it to neat piles. A couple of dozers cleared drives leading to the shuttered motels. People walked behind and to either side, shoveling what the dozers did not clear. There was a cheerful air to the scene, despite the task at hand.

Dillon watched them for a time, then turned around and started back uphill.

There had to be something he could do.

10

When Olivia entered the station's front room that next morning, Dillon was nowhere to be found. Porter and Maud stood in the same position as the previous day. Maud held an open file in one hand and jabbed at items on a page with her free hand. Porter frowned in concentration, shaking his head now and then, saying nothing. Then he spotted Olivia's approach and said, "Come save me from this nightmare."

"Well, thank you so very not at all," Maud snapped.

Porter asked, "Did Dillon speak with you?"

"About the portrait." Olivia nodded. "I'm happy to do it."

"It needs to be today. More rain is due, and Celia is packing up to leave."

"All right."

"Great." Porter reached for the phone. "I'll call the house and we'll set out."

Maud demanded, "What about these forms?"

"My standing here not understanding what you're telling me hasn't helped a bit." Porter punched in the number. "Do what you can and we'll hope for the best."

Maud loaned her a go-cup, which Olivia filled with coffee. She gathered her Canon and lenses and reflectors from her car, and was ready when Porter emerged and unlocked his pickup.

They held to silence as Porter drove them from town. Or rather, Olivia stayed quiet while Porter fielded several calls on his radio and one on his phone. She didn't understand what was being said, and really didn't care. They took another of the winding roads through a valley south of where she and Dillon had traveled. The going was almost identical, threading their way through piles of rubble gathered by the dozer gangs. Flashing lights marked where the road had been cut away. They took it slow.

Olivia had slept well, which she found mildly astonishing. She was not so much refreshed as able to calmly view her situation. This time spent in the jail was proving strangely helpful.

Olivia's early years had been defined by her desire to spread wings and fly away. Despite the love, the joy, the wonder her mother brought to most days. The cottage had often felt like nothing more than a cage perfumed by drying wildflowers.

And now that was gone.

In the light of another gray dawn, even if money wasn't such a critical factor, Olivia doubted she would ever rebuild the place. Make her mother's home her own. Somehow the concept just didn't fit.

Which brought her to the impossible situation she now faced.

Living with Dillon.

As friends.

Porter might as well have been reading her mind, for he chose that moment to say, "Your man took off early. Looked seriously worried about something."

"He's not . . . Don't call him that."

Porter glanced over. "Sorry."

"All that was over years ago. Now . . ." She sighed. "We're trying to find a new way forward. I don't know how to describe it any better."

"Makes sense," Porter said. "You want to be pals."

"We're that already," she replied. Now that they were talking, she found trying to frame it in words actually helped. "Last night we talked about rewriting the rule book. If we can."

He nodded. "People change. Relationships need to grow as well."

"There you go." She waited while Porter maneuvered them around a pair of dozers clearing the road. Once he exchanged waves with the drivers and accelerated, she went on, "The only thing that hasn't changed about Dillon is his need to work. Nothing makes that man sadder than standing still."

"Sounds like a guy after my own heart. He was in some kind of business, do I remember that right?"

"He had a small investment company. It went bust, but it wasn't his fault. I won't say any more because I'd probably get it wrong. Dillon trained as an accountant, then got a job on Wall Street . . ." She went quiet as Porter hit the brakes and pulled off the road. "What?"

Porter said, "Dillon's a bookkeeper and he's looking for work?"

"Probably best not to call him that. He was a lot more than your basic bookkeeper."

"Maud and I are too worried to split verbal hairs. Can the man handle red tape and numbers, is what I need to know."

"Porter, you need to ask him. But I'd say, absolutely. Why, you have a problem with your accounts?"

"Call it what it is. We're facing a full-blown crisis." He reached for his phone. "You really think he'd be willing to help us out?"

Something about the way Porter's frantic fingers had trouble working the phone brought up the day's first smile. "I know he'd like to try."

11

As Dillon approached the station, Maud shoved through the main doors and stomped her way across the parking lot. Dillon thought she looked like a drill sergeant on a tear. "Where on earth have you been?"

"Walking."

"How *dare* you slink off when there's work to do!"

"I have no idea what you're talking about."

"That's no excuse!" She waved one hand back at the station. "Disappearing today of all days! When the pile of official documents on your desk is a foot high!"

"*My* desk?"

She ignored his question. "Half my exhausted force has been out searching for your sorry hide!" She took hold of his sleeve and stomped back toward the entrance, dragging him along. "Can you or can you not understand a set of books?"

"Can." On definite ground. At least on that point.

"And you understand bureaucratic red tape?"

"Different question, same answer."

"So maybe Christmas won't miss us after all." A stray shaft of weak sunlight illuminated the glass portals as Maud pushed them open and declared, "The wayward lad has returned."

Ryan grinned at his confused state. "Guess we can call off the dogs."

Maud led him to the desk directly in front of hers. "Dillon, sit."

The desk was now piled with documents, folders, a tray of receipts, scrawled notes, and a desktop computer. "What is all this?"

"What does it look like?"

He opened the top folder, studied the spreadsheets, said, "A half-finished mess."

"Sounds like we've found our man," Ryan said. "Maybe you should deputize him."

"Can't hurt," Maud agreed. "Raise your right hand. Do you swear to uphold the law, behave yourself, get this work done on time, and not break Olivia's heart again?"

"What kind of oath is that?"

"Say yes," Maud declared. "That's an order."

"Okay, yes. But I didn't—"

"You just hush with that." For once, Maud's ire

became very real indeed. "Olivia's mother was one of my dearest lifelong friends. I helped her pack for the move to Phoenix. Your running away broke two beautiful hearts that day."

Dillon had no idea what to say.

Ryan offered a remarkably soft, "That was then and this is now."

Maud stood, hands on hips, glaring.

Ryan said, "Tell our new deputy what we're facing here." When Maud remained silent, she went on. "The state is offering us disaster-relief funding. Us, as in, the town and police and fire and emergency services. The problem is, nobody knows how to handle these forms."

Maud said, "Everybody is stretched impossibly thin. Even if we weren't, I doubt we could complete these on time."

"Maud is the best we have at red tape," Ryan said. "And she's overwhelmed. Just like the rest of us."

Dillon asked, "What's the due date?"

"Tomorrow," Maud replied. "Now get to work."

Fifteen minutes later, Dillon was as content as he'd been in what felt like forever.

The work was deeply complex and absorbing. Just the same, a portion of his mind was safe to drift back over the hard weeks and months he'd left behind.

Through the sleepless period of defeat and shame and futile struggle, he had lost touch with this. The joy he had always known while working.

Numbers like these formed a delicious puzzle. He could dive in, lose himself in piecing together the mystery that very few even realized was there. His ability had taken him so very far. And now brought him back to where he had started.

He broke the work into five segments. The state's jumble of paperwork and red tape came first, since that formed the necessary framework for everything else. Once he had a handle on the requirements, he launched into the four sets of books—police, fire, EMT, and all the equipment the town had leased from local contractors.

Hours passed.

Dillon was content. A kitten working its way through a saucer of double cream, with a silk cushion waiting by a roaring fire, had nothing on this guy.

A while later, he looked up to find a sandwich and steaming cup planted on the desk's corner. Only then did he realize how hungry he'd become. Dillon ate while doing a preliminary run-through of the fire station's books. Which were, in a word, a mess.

He fanned out reams of hand-scribbled notes, receipts that had been dashed off and smudged to oblivion, then dripped grainy mustard all over an email from the state confirming the highway department would reimburse them for clearing roads and using equipment normally reserved . . .

Dillon stopped when a shadow fell on the desk. He looked up to find Maud standing by his chair. Ryan was two steps back, observing. Dillon thought the detective had a lovely smile. "Yes?"

"The fire chief called. Do you want him to stop by?"

"Wouldn't hurt." His gaze was caught by a flicker of lightning. "It's raining."

Ryan chuckled, shook her head, turned away.

"Well, duh," Maud said.

Dillon thought the woman's glare had lost a touch of its former spice. "Thanks for the sandwich."

Ryan called from her desk, "You're welcome."

Maud asked, "You need anything?"

Lightning flashed, closer this time. "A laptop would help. You know, just in case we lose power. I can make sure nothing's lost . . ." He stopped talking when Maud turned and walked away. He caught sight of Ryan seated across the aisle, still grinning. "What?"

"Just wondering what that song was you kept humming."

This was news. "I don't hum."

Ryan laughed out loud.

"I can't carry a tune in a bucket."

She bent back over an open file. "You got that right."

Maud returned and set down a laptop and cables

beside his keyboard. "This is the chief's personal computer. You break it, you'll be back in the rear cell without a key."

The fire chief arrived soon after. Dillon wasn't exactly clear on timing. Which he took as a very good sign. The fire chief was a lean, rawboned man with craven features. He stripped off his yellow hazard gear, dragged over a chair, asked, "You mind?"

"Not at all."

He eased down like every joint hurt, then offered a meaty paw. "Charlie Hurst. Sorry about the mess we've dumped in your lap."

"It's okay, Chief. I figure you've done your best, given everything else you've had to handle."

The man's eyebrows were a pair of unkempt meadows. The eyes below were one shade darker than his skin. "That's not what I was expecting to hear from the man wading through my bad handwriting."

Dillon indicated the piles of receipts and scrawled notes. "Everything related to your fire stations is pretty clear. You've kept a running tally of all your daily operating expenses. What I haven't seen are summaries of your larger costs. I found a note saying you leased equipment from other sources, but I can't locate the charge sheets." Dillon picked up the yellow slips with nothing save a series of handwritten numbers. "You'll have to help me with these."

The chief took his time responding. "Maud told me you're the miracle worker we've been hoping for."

"I said no such thing." Maud rose from her desk. "Coffee?"

"Can't hurt." He told Dillon, "To answer your question, I've got an office full of charge sheets and receipts, and my copies of those things you write when you hope to pay off the kindness of strangers one day."

"Promissory notes?"

"Sounds right. My crews got saddled with a lot of the road work, basically because they volunteered and there wasn't anybody else. I keep trying to tell them you don't volunteer for nothing. But they've spent years learning to ignore me."

Dillon indicated the mostly handwritten pile. "So what I don't have here are things like . . ."

"Plows and dozers we rented from as far away as San Luis Obispo before the southern route got washed away." He squinted at the side wall, thinking. "Land we leased so we had somewhere to dump the rubble. Extra hands we hired. 'Bout a dozen other things I can't be bothered to recollect."

"What about hard-use amortization, damage to your own equipment, items that need replacing?"

"Yeah, I've done my best to keep up with that too. The main crews working the power lines are out of Santa Cruz. But we had some fellows down from

Frisco, and two of their trucks broke down. They've been using my ladder trucks. They aren't gentle."

"Okay, so there's no time to input all that," Dillon decided. "We'll make the split right here. What you've already supplied, we request payback from the state. Everything else we bundle into the FEMA application. That sound okay to you?"

Charlie Hurst accepted the mug from Maud without taking his eyes off Dillon. "You sure you understand what's required here?"

"Yes."

Maud took up station beside the fire chief. "He's been like that all day."

Charlie asked Dillon, "You really think the state auditors are going to accept a mess of notes in my bad writing, and pay us what we need?"

"They won't see any of this." Dillon swung his laptop around. "I'm inputting the figures into their form. Breaking down the costs by week."

"I didn't date the things. Didn't know I needed to."

"It doesn't matter. We have a series of bona fide expenses tied to an emergency situation. One so severe both the state and federal government have declared this a disaster area. The state auditor should take my forms and be grateful."

"You're certain of that, are you?"

"Absolutely."

Charlie took a noisy slurp. "What about this non-sense about submitting in the run-up to Christmas?"

"Makes perfect sense."

"Does it."

"Sure. Having the central coast declared a state and federal disaster area means two sets of financial floodgates are officially being opened. The state's set this supertight timeline so there's no overlap with the feds." Dillon fiddled with his trackpoint, brought up the second set of documents. "See here, the feds start their own giveaway program that very same day."

"Is that so."

"Right. FEMA will insist on inspecting the state request forms along with whatever we want to get from the feds, so they can make sure there's no double-billing. Which is where I'll need access to the receipts in your office."

Charlie glanced at Maud, took in her crossed arms and her frown, but all he said was, "What else can we ask the feds to pay for?"

"The coastal walk. That's top of my list." As Dillon drew up the relevant clause, Maud closed in tight beside the chief. "The walk, the road, the parking lot, the retainer wall, all this is covered by what they say here. If we can get some decent estimates in time, I want to include the motel entryways." Dillon hesitated, then added, "Maybe, if we do this right, we can get some money for the motels as well. Their gardens, the damage from hillside runoffs, treat it as infrastructure that plays a role in the town's enjoyment of the beachfront."

"You don't say."

"I can't promise that last bit. But yeah, that's what I'm hoping. And it's going to be submitted on time. Thanks to the great job Maud's done getting me started."

Charlie looked up at the station manager. "How can you stay mad at this guy?"

Maud snorted. "Don't get me started."

But Charlie wasn't having it. "Maud, apologize to the gentleman."

"No."

"Maud, I'm not asking you a second time."

"Since when did the likes of you . . ." But when Ryan walked over to stand on Charlie's other side, the station manager lost a good deal of her starch. She grumbled, then, "Oh, all right. I suppose you've earned a pass. But only if you get those documents off on time."

Charlie did his best to hide his smile. "I guess that will have to do."

12

Ten minutes after entering Porter's home, Olivia knew any decent portrait was going to require a struggle. Carol, his wife, and their daughter Celia were dressed in a countrified version of formal wear, stiff and uncomfortable and sad. Overhead Porter thumped around the bedroom, putting on the clothes Carol had laid out for him. The Christmas tree's lights were off, which she thought reflected the family's mood.

The kitchen was filled with fragrances from the roast in the oven, pots on the stove. Plates and utensils were stacked on the counter. Six of Celia's friends tossed a football in the damp yard between the main house and the barn. Two were local boys who also studied at UC Santa Cruz. The others had come down from university, here to celebrate a Miramar Christmas.

Ha.

Four dogs raced about, playing catch with strangers. Two SUVs were packed and ready to hit the road. Olivia watched them through the kitchen window, and thought they all shared the same unspoken sentiment.

When Porter came back downstairs, the three clustered together by the kitchen counter, stiff and formal and tired and stressed and sad. Their Christmas plans were in tatters. Their daughter was going away. The town was a mess. And it looked like the rain was going to start falling again, any minute now.

The only solution that came to Olivia was, take control.

"We have two choices." She did her best to sound both calm and matter-of-fact. "If you like, we can shoot a remembrance of what you're all feeling right now."

"Which is exactly what I *don't* want," Celia said.

"And you're worried that's all you're going to get," Olivia said. "One question. If this was a normal late morning, what would you be doing right now? Eleven fifteen on a good day."

Celia replied, "Feeding the horses. Trying to keep Daddy home long enough so we could go for a ride."

Carol added, "The vet has us feeding the colt a bottle with extra nutrients."

"Which we should be doing anyway," Porter said.

"I was saving that for after they eat and Celia leaves," Carol said. "Help me fill the empty hours."

Celia reached for her mom. Hugged her tight. "I'm so sorry."

"As if you're responsible for the weather."

"Maybe I could send them on. Stay and hope the roads—"

"No." Carol's voice held the iron-hard determination of a woman in control. Despite everything. "Don't let's start. Again."

Porter watched his two ladies and sighed.

Olivia said, "Why don't we move over to the barn and try a few pictures there?"

"I can't leave the stove untended," Carol replied. "I'm in the middle of preparing our final meal together as a family."

Celia said, "Let my friends take over."

"In my kitchen? Not on your bippy."

Their daughter pointed out the window. "Mom, three of those people are trained chefs."

"Correction. They're short-order cooks."

"At Santa Cruz's oceanfront diner. They're studying business to start their own premier restaurant."

"That's as may be. Right now they're still fry-up lads."

"Daddy, tell her."

"I'm not dancing to that tune," her father replied. "Remember, I have to live here after you're gone."

Olivia said, "What I'm hoping is, if we do something that's a normal part of a normal day, we can get something that you'd be happy with."

"Mom, please. She's right and you know it."

"I'll never find anything in here ever again."

"And dress like you would normally," Olivia added. "Clean and comfortable barn clothes. Happy clothes."

"Now you're talking." Porter stripped off his tie, shrugged out of his jacket. "I can breathe again."

"I thought you looked nice," Carol complained.

"We can go for the formal look on another day," Olivia said. "Hurry before the sky goes dark again."

Olivia scouted the barn while Porter ushered their guests indoors and the ladies changed. At her request, Porter opened the barn's two skylights that had been shut against the storm. The resulting light, she decided, was almost perfect.

When the ladies arrived, she was ready. "Porter, I'm sorry but you need to take off that Stetson."

"Celia won't let me have my picture taken wearing the police cap."

"You need to have your head bare for the pictures. In this gray light your face would be completely masked, and I want to shoot without flash."

He reluctantly hung his hat from a nail. "Now I'm almost naked."

Celia and her mom wore jeans, checked shirts, and

high-heeled boots. Carol tied a kerchief around her daughter's neck and said, "I'd pay good money to have a picture of Porter in his altogether."

"Don't you even start," Porter said. "Else I'll think you've been out here with my daughter and her pals, smoking the evil weed."

"I never," Celia said. "Mom, that scarf is too tight."

"It's perfect. Now hold still while I fix your hair."

The passion was filling Olivis now. The flame she feared had gone out forever, snuffed from existence by all the hard nights. Instead, here she was in a live action situation, her favorite venue. It did not matter that Porter almost danced in place with nervousness, or how his wife's face remained shadowed by the storm and her daughter's pre-Christmas departure. All that was secondary, if Olivia were able to make this work. Which she would. Despite everything.

"Why don't I start with your daughter and the colt. We can shoot the family portrait when things calm down."

She actually saw the two parents take an easy breath. Porter said, "Shame the light's so gloomy."

"Actually, it's grand. Carol, untie the colt and bring him up here where I'm standing. Good. See how that puts his head directly in the light? Okay, Porter, take this reflector. Come stand where I'm pointing and direct it at the colt's head."

"I have no idea how to do what you're saying. This reflector thing doesn't have a scope."

"Hold it with two hands like you would a steering wheel. Now look straight at the colt and aim it where you're looking." She shifted back to where she intended to shoot and looked through the camera. "No, that's too far over. Back up half a pace. Perfect. Now, Celia, step over so you're on the colt's other side. Can you make the animal stop bobbing its head?"

"I can groom the mane. He'll hold still for hours if I do that."

"Great. Can you please shift ten inches to your left? Good. Now angle your body, no, not your head. Shift your body without moving your feet . . . Right there." She motioned to Carol. "Come have a look."

"Oh my sweet heavens above. Porter, honey, you've got to see this."

"He can't. He's busy. He'll see it later." Olivia shot a dozen images, then, "Carol, why don't you go take hold of the reins. Good. Now turn slightly to your right, no, keep your feet where they are. Shoulder down. No, your other shoulder."

"Why do I feel like a storefront mannequin?"

"Hush now, Mom. The lady's on a roll."

"Celia, hold that smile. Great. Carol, why don't you take the brush and curry the mane between his ears. Excellent." She shot several pictures, then said,

"Porter, set down that reflector and go join the ladies. You need to get in closer to your daughter. That's it. Just lean in to her, otherwise the shadows . . . Perfect." Ten shots later, Olivia decided to go with a flash. "Carol, take a firm hold on those reins, the colt may be startled." She angled the flash straight up, so as to minimize the effect while still illuminating the scene. "Okay, Porter, you can take half a step back. A smidgen more." Three more shots, then, "Now step over so you're right in close with your wife, good. Celia, can you lean toward your parents, like you want to hug them but can't?"

"I feel like that almost every day I'm away."

Carol's voice caught. "Oh, honey."

Olivia shot so fast she lost count, then, "I think that does it."

Despite the rain and wind and gloom and Porter's slow progress, Olivia carried a happy vibe back to the station. She didn't need to wait for a closer inspection of her photographs. She knew in her heart the pictures were first-rate. Once she had made her selection and printed and framed, it might not make up for a daughter missing Christmas. But it would help. Of that she was certain.

Porter's mind was apparently following a similar path, for he chose that moment to say, "You did us all a world of good back there."

"I'm glad." She decided happy wasn't the proper way to describe this moment. She was still weighed down by everything that had brought her here. Not to mention a cottage that would probably never be her home again. Or how she was traveling back to spend another night in the town jail.

Not to mention that other thing. How, once the roads opened up, she would be playing roomies with the man who broke her heart.

Yes indeed. Definitely a Christmas for the books.

Porter reached over, switched off the police radio, and asked, "So how does a lady from Miramar become a big-time professional down in LA?"

"I was never one of those celebrity photographers. You know, name in lights, chased by the stars, that sort of thing."

Porter's smile was weighed down by everything the man carried. But it still warmed the moment. "Oh, go on. Tell me about the stars you met. Name some names."

"I never do. That was one reason why I became trusted by the producers. See, while a film is being shot, the producers try their best to generate good press. They hire a PR team and a photographer. My job was to make the team look happy while they made a great film." She leaned her head back, remembering. "My ex gave me my first big break. The photographer he normally used came down with

Covid, and he asked me to fill in. He and the director liked my work enough to start using me on a regular basis. Word got around."

"All of a sudden, your star was on the rise."

"Something like that. Eventually I had the chance to work with a few older stars. I loved that. They're constantly worried about being shot when not at their best. You've heard the LA adage for female actors? As they age, they're shunted from playing the hot babe to district attorney to Driving Miss Daisy. It's during that last phase when my work was most important. These aging actors love their work and want to keep going, which means finding someone they can trust to only share pictures that show them at their very finest."

Porter waved to someone she couldn't be bothered to see. "And here you are now, back in little Miramar, photographing a cop and his clan."

She heard the unspoken question, knew he was offering her a chance to deflect. "My ex ran off with a floozy. I know that word is out of fashion. But that's exactly what she was. I was certain that was a short-run fling, long before she left him for a stuntman on a steroid diet."

Porter did his best to keep his laughter inside, and failed. "Sorry. That slipped out."

"Then the strikes hit the industry, my ex's company went bankrupt, the film world shut down. I hung on as long as I could, but in the end I lost my home and everything else. And came back just in time to watch where I hoped to live slide off the hillside."

Porter didn't speak again until he entered the station parking lot, cut the motor, and shifted in his seat so as to face her. "You're part of this town. You've got friends here. We take care of our own. We'll help you see your way through this. I don't know how to say it any plainer than that."

13

Olivia entered the station to find Dillon seated at the desk directly in front of Maud's. He was heads down, so intent on his work the rest of the world might as well just float away. The desk was blanketed with forms and handwritten pages and smudged slips of paper. The sight took her straight back. The young kid who escaped from his awful home long before she fashioned her own getaway. So involved in whatever challenge he set for himself, the young Dillon did not even pay attention to the school's bullies. A handsome kid in hand-me-down clothes, clean because his grandmother insisted on doing their laundry. Nor did he care. He remained focused on doing well, honing his gifts, finding identity in whatever job was cast his way. Just like now.

Olivia spoke a few words, just to reconnect and make sure he was okay. But she doubted he was fully aware of her standing there. Then she went back outside and settled her gear in the trunk. The rain had diminished to a mist only slightly finer than fog. A gentle breeze blew salt-laden spray. She zipped up her rain gear and set off walking.

Miramar's main street was less crowded than on the afternoon of her arrival. The parking areas were much less full, and fewer families walked aimlessly along the sidewalks. But tattered Christmas decorations still dangled from wires and poles and storefronts. Most streetlights remained off, and few of the shopfront windows were illuminated.

In a way, she shared Dillon's attitude. Working on the photographs had left her shielded from the gray afternoon. As she descended Ocean Avenue's gentle slope, Olivia decided she had been wrong to call herself happy. The season was too fractured for such a word. It was only when she stood in front of the camera store and saw her framed portrait of the jail-cell family there in the shop window that a different word came to mind. One that suited her like a tailored suit.

She was *content*.

Olivia could see Gleason dealing with another customer, so she remained where she was, standing in the rainswept shopping street, admiring her work. Rain streaking the glass made by the family come alive, especially the children. It was good work. She had done this. Despite everything the world had thrown at her. The longer she stood there, the more certain she became that this was, without doubt, a true Christmas gift. One that would help her through the seasons yet to come.

Gleason greeted her with a look that took Olivia straight back. The rumpled overweight bear of a man with a scowl to match. "I suppose you'll be wanting your money."

For a long moment she had no idea what he was talking about. Then, "The photograph in your window. You sold it."

"Not the print. That's mine. But two magazines have bought rights to publish it. I had to push like crazy. Those editors wouldn't know art if it bit them."

She realized Gleason was angling for a commission. The fact that he wouldn't come straight out was oddly touching. "I've never had an agent before. I'd be honored if you'd work with me."

The older man seemed momentarily at a loss. Then, "How did you find jobs in LA?"

"I became known to some producers and directors. They booked me on a pretty regular basis. Then a couple of older stars started calling me for casual-style PR shots. Not many. But some."

"And you grew up in the process." He banged open the old-fashioned cash register, passed over a check. "I've sold your photo to *California Styles*. *Mother Jones* is using it for their next cover. Your work bumped the governor to next month."

The check was for two and a half thousand dollars. Olivia breathed around the enormity of what she held. "Gleason . . ."

"The Santa Cruz paper wants it but they haven't said how much. I haven't heard back from LA yet. I've been told they take forever."

"You've done this in a *day*."

He pretended at unconcern, but Olivia could see he was very proud. "Just so happened both journals are giving the storms a lot of coverage."

"This is enormous." She looked up. "Is this minus your commission?"

"Glad you asked. And the answer is no, since we haven't reached an agreement. Ten percent sound about right?"

"Absolutely." She tried to hand it back.

"No, no, I'll just take it out of whatever else comes in."

She pocketed the check. The paper felt warm as a live coal to her fingers. "Speaking of which, I have the results of a new shoot. I need some prints."

He was already moving. He locked the front door, put the sign in place telling customers to ring the bell, then said, "Come on around back."

Entering Gleason's secret domain took Olivia straight back. She had been borderline terrified the first time this gruff old man had invited her. The back room was huge, far larger than the shop itself. She walked slowly down the central aisle, surrounded by shelves reaching up to the ceiling, many of them glass fronted, all of them carefully dusted and polished. They held a treasure trove of camera history. The apparatus dated back to photography's earliest days, when several mules were required to carry the bulky cameras and their glass plates.

Originally this room had been sectioned into four. But the development machines that had once created a lab-like atmosphere were all replaced now by computer-driven efficiency. The walls had been torn out, and this mini-museum to California's photographic history was created. Olivia paused by the line of enlargers and development tanks and drying cabinets, remembering what it was like to make her very first adult friend.

When she looked up, Gleason showed her a surprisingly gentle smile. "You always were my finest unpaid assistant."

She was tempted to reply, *And look where it brought me*. But remained silent.

He eased himself down into a wooden swivel chair dating from the same era as his former darkroom. It creaked in protest as he pulled in close. "Grab a chair." Olivia had heard those very same words any number of times. They no longer carried the thrill of earlier days, when the young teen was enthralled with her newfound abilities, and heard in Gleason's invitation a chance to enter the professional ranks. Someday. Perhaps.

Gleason's computerized system was superb, three giant monitors, the left one poised vertically, while others held to the standard horizontal position. Only now the taller screen showed Olivia's jail-cell portrait beneath the cover of the *Los Angeles Times* Sunday magazine. "You can't be serious."

"Don't get your hopes up. This is a mockup. I wanted to show them where I thought they should put it. Nothing more." He erased the image and held out his hand. "Let's have your drive." He inserted the mini-card into the reader, then picked up a pair of reading glasses from the desk. When her stream of photos filled the taller screen, he asked, "Which of these do you want?"

He used the same software as Olivia, which would help enormously if she had something useable. "I came straight from the shoot and haven't inspected them yet. Why not scroll through in order, and I'll make note of any that work."

Gleason slid a pad and pen, brought up the first photo, grunted in surprise, said, "You've been working with Porter's family."

"Their daughter leaves today for college. Grad school issues. She couldn't risk . . ." Olivia stopped because Gleason was watching her, not the screen. "What?"

He examined her a moment longer. The dark eyes peered with gentle intensity over the top of his reading glasses. Then he turned back and began running through the photographs. Slowly, slowly.

Mother and daughter and colt merged into a happy-sad collage. The light was a gentle hand, a stroke of loving illumination. The two ladies seemed to glow with all the emotions of a fractured season.

"Olivia . . ."

Porter entered the scene. As she had hoped, Celia's father remained an almost-hidden figure. Shadows were draped over his solid form, with only his face fully illuminated. He was an incredibly strong man, capable of defying the gloom, sheltering his family with all he was, everything he had to give.

Olivia decided, "The black-and-white structure works best here. The old-fashioned silver-backed application, I like the way it sets the family. It gives them timeless appeal." Olivia liked the clinical tone she heard in her voice. The ability to study, assess, improve, grow. Even now, when she was so engaged with this new work. "But when I think back on my early years here, what I remember most are the colors. Our region is filled with some of the most vividly beautiful light on earth." She tapped the screen. "This is real, and this is now. But one day soon, I want to start doing portraits where color is as real a character as the people."

Gleason slipped the spectacles from his face. His fingers were a bit unsteady as he tapped the desk top. Silent. Thinking.

Olivia was more than willing to wait with him. The moment offered her an uncommon chance to inspect this gruff old man. It was tempting to think there was nothing beneath his scowling exterior. But seated here in this openhearted state, drawn together by the work she had accomplished with her talents and her camera, she saw how Gleason carried the same shadows as everyone else in Miramar. And there too was a singular joy. The same paradox of impossible emotions that she herself felt.

"My wife is senior nurse at what passes for the Miramar hospital." Gleason's voice had dropped a full octave. "She has a hundred reasons to be grateful for Porter serving as our chief of police. A thousand." Unsteady hands used the mouse to scroll back to what was undoubtedly Olivia's own favorite photo of the three. "She's going to take one look at this and bawl."

She wiped her own cheeks, then patted the man's shoulder. Determined to thank him just as soon as her voice returned.

*   *   *

When Olivia left the shop, clouds and rain dominated their world. The hour of dusk was a trivial matter. The sky was blanketed, the light very dim. Somewhere in the distance the ocean roared a constant warning of stronger storms to come.

In the gloom and damp the streets and sidewalks were almost empty. As she passed the shuttered Castaways restaurant, Olivia realized she was very hungry. But there was a line filling the diner's front space and crowding the register, so she took the side alley, went around back, and knocked on the open door. "Any chance I can sneak in for more rat stew?"

"We're all out of rats." Her oldest friend scurried into view, tired and flushed and happy as usual. "It's down to snakes and lizards this evening."

"We ate the last of those hours ago!" Arnaud pointed a spoon at a passing dishwasher. "You! Go find a stray armadillo!"

"Hi, Arnaud."

"You need to stop by for a real meal once life gets sane. Meet our little boy. Whose name I'll remember one of these days." He lifted the lid on a huge stewpot and his face was lost to a whirl of steam. But not his voice. Or his cheer. "At our home, not our nuthouse of a diner."

"This nuthouse is about to pay off our bank loan."

Claire pointed Olivia to a stool. "Sit. Relax. I'll be back."

Five minutes later Claire returned with two steaming plates. "You reminded me I need to eat."

"What about Arnaud?"

Her husband replied, "I steal food off everybody's plate. Perks of the job."

Tonight's one-plate special was a sweet-and-sour vegetarian delight, served on a bed of wild rice. "This is amazing."

"My dear sweet impossible man was made for a crisis like this." Claire tasted. "Not bad."

"It's fabulous, Arnaud."

"Yeah, I hit it pretty close to decent tonight. If only I wasn't winging it and could remember what I put in when."

Olivia asked between bites, "Why is that restaurant down the way shut?"

"Castaways. Sylvie Cassick's place. She arrived after you fled the scene. You'll love her. And her husband." Claire pretended to swoon.

"Handsome?"

Arnaud shouted, "He's not so great."

"Connor Larkin," Claire said.

"Wait, the movie star?"

"And he can sing." Claire rolled her eyes. "One of their twins has a thing. A twist in the intestines, was what Sylvie said. They left for the San Francisco children's hospital before the big storm and got stuck. Two days later the Castaways assistant manager came down with the never-get-overs and they closed for the holidays."

"I thought I saw a lot fewer vehicles on the streets tonight."

Arnaud stopped by for a bite from his wife's plate. "The morning news claimed they were finally clearing the northern passes."

Claire swatted his hand. "And the valley highway east to Paso Robles."

Arnaud tasted, rocked his head side to side. "It's missing something."

"Go complain over your own meal!"

"That's no fun." To Olivia, "Yes, part of the roads have been cleared. And no, not totally. Some families facing a longer trek are holding back. Especially now that there are rooms at the only inn still open."

"Steal more of my food and you'll be cooking with one hand, mister!" When Arnaud returned to his stoves, Claire asked, "So you'll be moving into the guesthouse?"

"Tell the truth, I'm happy where I am. And it's not for too long."

Claire stopped eating. "I heard your cottage isn't in great shape."

"Terrible," Olivia agreed. She hesitated, then decided it would be better if Claire heard it from her.

"Dillon's grandparents' old place is okay. Soon as the water and power are back, he's moving in. He's offered me a room."

All kitchen noise stopped.

Arnaud popped back into view as Claire said, "So. You and Dillon."

"Don't you start."

"If he and Connor were to run for Miramar's hottest, it would be a close call."

"I heard that!" Arnaud drifted closer, asked Olivia, "More?"

"Another half portion would be great." To Claire, "I'm still scalded by everything I left behind in LA. We're talking, serious burn victim."

Claire lost her smile. "It's really nice to have you back. Sorry about the reasons."

"Dillon is being a nice, sweet, gentle friend." Olivia faced the corkboard and its myriad of recipes, bills, notices, Christmas cards, scrawled notes. As if she could find a script that might explain the confusion she felt over hearing his name. "I know what it sounds like. But it doesn't *feel* that way."

To their credit, Arnaud remained silent and Claire did not tease. Her oldest friend asked, "What does it *feel* like?"

"Like he's helping me get my feet back on the ground." Olivia saw the same warm intelligence, the no-nonsense gaze, the inner beauty that had carried them both through so much. "Like he feels the same way I do. Like our romance is part of ancient history. That was then and this is now."

Claire gave that a moment. "You better be certain Dillon agrees on that point. Because if you're wrong, moving into his place would be pulling the pin on a live grenade."

14

Dillon worked through much of the night. Olivia returned at some point, he wasn't sure when. Her cheeks were flushed, her hair and clothes dripping wet. The brilliant light was back in her gaze, along with a smile that looked for reasons to spring into view. Like so many grand times they had known together. Back in the day.

Dillon granted himself a single moment to remember, and another to speak with her when she emerged from the showers. She was dressed in police sweats with a towel wrapped around her hair. Olivia spoke of a good day spent trying to take photographs of Porter's family despite the rain and fractured season. Dillon wasn't sure of what exactly he said in response. But it must have been the right words, because later she brought him a plate of food and smiled and said he looked happy as well. Which he was. Very.

There were any number of missing components. Which was mostly what took him so long. There was a great deal of guesswork and estimations to be included. But he needed to remain within the boundaries of reality. These state auditors were no fools. They might be sitting on a pile of money, ready to dole out their version of a Christmas bonus. But these auditors knew the difference between hard-fought costs and pure fantasy. So Dillon checked and rechecked, and argued with himself, and prepared the best he could.

When he was fairly certain the required documents were as ready as they would ever be, he shared them with Maud. For once, her grouchy bark remained silent. Instead, she heard him out, phoned Porter, spoke too quietly for Dillon to hear, then reached for a pen and signed.

Just the same, Dillon spent hours reviewing his work. For the sake of his former hometown, he had to get this right.

When he finally emailed the forms to Sacramento, the station was silent. A lone duty officer leaned back in her chair, watching the rain. She offered a casual wave in response to Dillon's weary goodnight.

The corridor back to his lonely cell seemed endless.

Dillon stopped by Olivia's cell and spent a long moment watching her sleep. There was a distinct comfort in sharing this moment with his oldest friend. Finally he entered the drunk tank, stripped down to his boxers, fell onto his pallet, searched in the dark for his blanket, gave up, and was gone.

15

The next thing Dillon knew, Olivia was kneeling by his pallet. Maud stood in the doorway, not exactly frowning. Just being Maud. Which was definitely an improvement.

"You snore," Olivia told him.

"That's why you woke me up? To say I'm making noise?"

"This goes way beyond noise," she replied. "Sit up and take this."

"This" was a steaming mug. The smell of coffee pushed him upright. "I could use another couple of hours."

Maud asked, "What time did you finish last night?"

"I didn't check the clock. Late." He realized a pair of blankets were tangled about his form. "Where did these come from?"

"The Christmas elf," Maud replied, and started

back down the corridor. "You've got twenty minutes."

He asked Olivia, "What's happening?"

"Things have been kicked up a level." Olivia rose
to her feet. "Better get a move on."

Dillon entered the station's main room to the
sound of laughter defying the day's gray light. Porter
and the fire chief and a younger officer stood with
their backs to him, blocking Dillon's view of whoever
was causing the mirth. Olivia stood by the kitchenette's entry, smiling and . . .

Happy.

Her face shone with a light that took him straight
back. The young lady at her best was visible again, a
magical California sprite who could light up the
darkest hour. Turn a troubled young man from the
problems and worries that dwelled in his home and
heart. Fill him with a momentary joy over simply
being alive and in her company.

He stood there at the periphery of whatever was
happening. His mind flashed back to the first time he
had seen her as more than just the childhood pal from
down the hill. Olivia had been a year ahead of him in
school, as her birthday was two weeks over the
boundary line and his was three weeks behind. Something she loved to bring up, how she was the elder in
their relationship. On that particular day, Dillon had
entered the school and not seen her, but rather how

all the faces within view were aimed in the same direction. They had seemed to reflect a magical illumination, and a desire to capture the flame.

But she had chosen him, the kid with no future.

Occasionally he had become captured by the fear that Olivia chose him simply because he needed her more than anyone else. Which had been both shameful and true . . .

Then the group shifted position, and Dillon's focus shifted to the woman who held their attention.

Growing up, Bailey Long had been the woman named most likely to do whatever she wanted in life. In Bailey's case, it was stay in Miramar and take care of whatever needed doing. Lead from the front, that was Bailey in a nutshell.

Their senior year was also the point when Bailey had fallen head over heels in love with Dillon's best friend.

Dillon had often thought Griff Gaines was an odd choice as Bailey's lifetime mate. Griff was as easygoing as Bailey was intense. A good-natured fellow who could stop any schoolyard battle with a smile. Which was how they had been brought together, after Griff had been named the school's head marshal. Griff and Dillon had both found the appointment hilarious, seeing as how they had played a lead role in so many earlier pranks. But Griff had grown into the position, bringing an astonishing level of peace and harmony to their final year. Especially after he and Bailey hooked up, and Griff was given another reason to outgrow his Peter Pan years.

Porter said, "I don't guess introductions are needed."

"Long time, Dillon," Bailey said. "You look . . ."

"Strung out and battered," Dillon suggested, and accepted a refreshed mug.

"I was going to say, all grown up. But I suppose your words will do."

"Sort of defines the season," Maud offered.

Olivia said, "The diner's brought us a plate of breakfast burritos."

"Which the chief wanted to snarf, right down to the very last crumb," Charlie said.

"Now we both know that's not true," Porter said. "I was only kidding about that last one."

"I had to beat him off with a rolling pin," Maud said.

Bailey had the remarkable ability to stand at the center of everything, and yet remain politely distant. Her expression took Dillon straight back, the smile, the piercing gaze, the quiet authority. Dillon had always thought of her as a general in waiting. Never more than now. He accepted a still-warm burrito and asked, "Why am I here?"

Ten minutes later, Dillon was seated at his desk, holding his recharged mug in one hand while pointing to the laptop's screen. He explained decisions he'd made late the night before, now imbedded into the state's forms as numbers. Concrete requests for urgent financial assistance. Helping a town planted on the storm's front line.

Porter and the fire chief frowned at his words, clearly having trouble following his explanation. Bailey's response was entirely different. She watched Dillon as much as the electronic charts. Studying him with something that almost looked like approval.

Charlie Hurst asked Porter, "You understand what this fellow's saying?"

"Not in a year of Sundays," Porter replied. "Not if I stood here 'til next Christmas."

"Doesn't matter," Bailey said, straightening. "He sounds like a pro. That's going to make as much difference as numbers on the screen."

Porter remained bent over, squinting. "Sure about that, are you?"

"I am, yes." She checked her watch. "Two minutes to showtime."

"You men need to shift to your stations," Maud said. "Everybody else, stay out of range and keep quiet."

"Good luck," Olivia told Dillon, and followed Ryan into the kitchenette.

"I won't be needing a desk," the mayor replied. "Maud, scooch me over an empty chair. I'm going to sit here behind our star player, make sure he sings on tune."

"Your confidence is just so reassuring," Dillon said.

As the two men shifted to empty desks, Charlie said, "Somebody's got to hook me up here."

"That makes two of us," Porter said. "With my daughter at university I can't hardly work the coffee-maker."

"You men," Maud said. She moved from one desk to the next. "Dillon, you need me to hold your hand?"

"Our lad's already up and running." Bailey had her phone out, typing swiftly. "Maud, you should join in on this."

"I'm not on the approved list."

"Sign in using my name." Bailey kept typing. "If Ransom objects, I'll explain. But I doubt he'll even notice."

Dillon asked, "Ransom?"

"Ransom Bates. State auditor. Not our pal." Bailey showed the remarkable ability to talk and type at hyper-speed. "My predecessor was part of a state-wide scam that Ransom missed. When it became public, Ransom got publicly splashed with mud."

"The man deserved a lot worse," Maud said. "He should have been locked up with all the others."

Bailey tsk-tsked. "It would not be in the town's

best interests for their mayor to say the state auditor had his head buried in the sand."

Dillon asked, "Who are you texting?"

"Just a pal in Sacramento." She checked the message, hit send, and pocketed the phone. "In case Ransom decides this is his chance to get even."

Abruptly Dillon was captured by a memory. The last time he had been seated in such a position, prepared to pitch a financial document with calm confidence, had been his downfall. Lured by lies into believing he had found a huge opportunity, so big he pitched it with confidence to his fund's primary investors. They would all go in big, and come out rich.

If only.

He wished for the screen to come alive, give him a reason to push away the bitter regret. But the main screen remained blank except for the message that they waited for the meeting's leader. Dillon turned to the woman seated at his right and said, "So. Mayor Bailey."

"Actually, it's Mayor Long."

Which carried the jolt required to shove the memories aside. Griff's last name was Gaines, and Bailey wore no ring.

Since Dillon had served as Griff's best man at their wedding, he searched for something proper and came up blank.

But Bailey showed him that slightly canted grin of hers, and said, "Go for it, sport."

"No Griff?"

"Not for years. Which you would know, if you'd stayed in touch."

He nodded. "Guilty."

She liked that. "See, that's the difference between you and my ex. Griff never found an uncomfortable moment he couldn't run from."

"I reached out to Griff several times. He only wrote back once. A two-word text. 'Don't ask.'"

"Sounds like Griff." She managed to hold on to her grin. "Now's your chance to say how you never thought we were a match made in heaven."

Which were precisely the words he had spoken to Griff at the bachelor party.

Dillon shook his head. "I'm carrying too many bad moves of my own to comment on anybody else's errors in judgment."

She asked, "Are you staying or passing through?"

"Nowhere else to go."

"Truth or Christmas fable?"

"I ran a smallish investment fund. I pointed my investors to a huge new opportunity called Lead Balloon Incorporated. I lost everything. Including my reputation and any chance I had of ever starting over."

"I'm so sorry, Dillon. You deserved better." Then the laptop pinged. Instantly Bailey stowed away her patent-perfect smile and aged ten years. She said loud enough for all the station to hear, "Okay, people. Here we go."

16

When Ransom Bates finally appeared on screen, the word that came to Dillon's mind was *prune*. The guy was probably still in his forties. And his face remained relatively unlined. Just the same, his expression was stamped with an indelible negative. As if he had been denied what he most wanted as a child, and was going to spend the rest of his life making everyone pay.

The first words out of his mouth were, "Your numbers don't add up."

Dillon had worked with prunish accountants all his life. People who entered into every dialogue expecting to be scammed. Whose greatest joy in life came from saying no.

Bailey asked, "Can you please give me a for instance?"

"I don't need to. And I don't have the time to teach you people rudimentary accounting." He scanned the faces frowning back at him, Bailey and Maud and Charlie and Porter and Dillon. "Your requests for state funding are hereby denied—"

He was silenced by a computer ping. A sixth face popped into view. The dark-skinned gentleman was portly and grinning and wearing a peaked Santa's hat. "Ho, ho, ho."

Bailey said, "Boyd Harrow, what a surprise."

Ransom snorted his disbelief, but quietly. If anything his expression grew even more severe.

Bailey went on. "Everyone, this is my pal Boyd, formerly head of Standard Charter, currently serving as the governor's chief of staff. Boyd, meet everyone."

"Bailey, how are you and that lovely town of yours holding up?"

"Touch and go, Boyd. Depends on the day. We appreciate the state's help."

"More with every passing hour," Porter added.

"Well, we're here to serve the greater good. Isn't that right, Ransom?"

Dillon could almost hear the state auditor's teeth grinding.

"I've taken a look at your documents, and so has the governor's bookkeeper. We both feel there's a real case for your getting everything you've requested."

Ransom started, "Actually, sir, there are some very serious issues—"

"Did you just interrupt me?" Boyd lost his smile.

When Ransom remained grimly silent, the governor's top man continued. "Oh, good. I was concerned about a serious breach of protocol. Now where was I?"

"I'm not sure," Bailey replied. "Suddenly I went all breathless."

"Money. That's right. Look, here's what I propose. We are going to deposit all the requested funds into your town's account this afternoon. When the sun comes out again, we'll sit around the table and hammer out the details. That sound good to you, Ransom?"

The state auditor remained mute. Motionless.

"Excellent." Boyd was clearly enjoying himself. "So you will *personally* contact my office and *assure* me the funds have gone out *before close of business.* We clear on that, Ransom?"

"Sir." The man sounded positively strangled.

"Good. Sorry, people. I'm off to put my finger in another dike. Merry Christmas and all that."

Bailey waited for the governor's man to sign off before telling the auditor, "Thank you for your time."

Ransom's response was cut off by the screen going blank. Dillon was glad he hadn't actually heard the words.

Bailey said again, "Breathless."

Right then, with a sigh from the furnace as it went quiet, the lights went out. Porter's radio squawked first, then the fire chief's. Charlie reported, "Whole town's just gone dark again."

Sullen gray light filtered through the station windows, illuminating the group as they rose and unlimbered. Maud said, "Shame that good feeling couldn't have lasted a trace longer."

"Oh, I don't know." Bailey offered Dillon a grand smile. "Thanks to our man here, my day has been made. Power or no power."

Dillon said, "Before your friend in Sacramento showed up, I thought we were done for."

"Yeah, it helps to have pals in high places." Bailey pointed at the front door. "Why don't you and I go for a ride, I'll show you where we'd most like to have the feds help us out with the rebuilding process."

Bailey drove a white Tahoe along Ocean Avenue, taking her time, then swung around the park and meandered through two residential areas. Now and then she stopped and spoke with people—power company technicians repairing a line, driver of an ER vehicle, an elderly couple making hard going of the rubble-strewn sidewalk.

Dillon enjoyed seeing the grown-up Bailey interact with her town. She held the gentle authority of a good general, her strength and severity well hidden. But there just the same. Given a hard moment where anger was justified, Dillon was certain this woman could scorch the earth.

Which probably explained why she wore no ring.

Growing up, her ex had been a perfect foil for Dillon's desperate impatience. Griff defined easygoing. He was not lazy, far from it. But Griff had been born with no ambition whatsoever. He accepted Dillon's single-minded focus, just as he did his wife's steely motivation. But Griff never truly understood either. He surfed, he fished, he worked with the crews building his family's next construction project. He was the only son of a wealthy real estate developer, and made no bones about spending every free day doing exactly what he wanted.

Bailey returned to the car, started the motor, said for the fourth time, "Sorry about these interruptions."

"I like watching the mayor at work." He waited while she paused for a quick word with another crew, then asked, "Where is Griff these days?"

"Running his family's resort hotel down in Cabo." She turned right into Ocean Avenue and continued downhill. "It's his idea of a perfect life. He has a great staff, they do almost everything. Griff shows up when he wants, signs the checks. The best fishing in the world, nice waves, warm water, happy tourists down for a good time." The smile she tossed him was half a lie. "He couldn't believe it when I said I wouldn't leave Miramar and join him."

"When was this?"

"Five and a half years ago. I'm surprised he didn't invite you down for his fun-filled version of paradise."

"I started my own company around that same time. I let a lot of things slide. Too many, for too long."

"By that point, our happy family was already falling apart. Had been for a couple of years." Bailey's words held a matter-of-fact calm. Water under the dam. "Griff's parents accepted the reality long before we could. Offering Griff this job was their way of helping us out of an impossible situation."

"I'm so sorry."

They didn't speak again until Bailey pulled into the oceanfront lot and parked by the yellow warning tape. "Go for a walk?"

They started down the beachfront road. This close to the Pacific, the mist was heavily spiced with brine. The fog gently billowed off the ocean, coating every surface. If Bailey even noticed she gave no sign. The ocean was calm, the day very still. A gentle, almost apologetic rain fell, punctuated by the cries of gulls. Dillon told her, "Maud thinks there's another big storm on the way."

"The latest weather report isn't so definite. I hope she's wrong for once." Bailey stopped in front of the remnants of the first walking bridge. All that was left were three tall pilings, jutting out of the mist like monuments to past happy days. "Tell me how you think we should proceed with FEMA."

Dillon nodded. He'd been mentally working on this since leaving the station. "I take it the feds don't have a ceiling on what you can ask for?"

"I have no idea. This is a first for Miramar. But my guess is, we should ask for everything, because that is exactly what we really need, and hope for the best."

"So we describe our crisis situation one step at a time. Break it down into bite-size chunks." He gestured at the broken bridge. "For each item, we give them before-and-after images. Maybe you could ask Olivia to help with those. She'll make the crisis live for the people who've never been here."

"I like this. A lot." Bailey pointed them back to her ride. "Why don't we go dry off."

When they were seated, she turned both the AC and the heater on high. Then sat there, watching the wipers swing in a futile attempt to clear the scene. "So. You and Olivia."

Dillon leaned against the side door, happy to sit there all day. "We arrived back in Miramar on the same day, pretty much."

Bailey remained intent on the gray-wrapped day. "Single and ready to rekindle the old fire."

"Single, yes. Ready, no."

She looked at him. "That's not what people are saying."

"I can imagine."

"It's not true?"

"I haven't discussed it with the lady in question." Easy with the conversation. Glad to be discussing it with such a trusted friend. "But for me, no, that's not how it feels."

"How does it feel, Dillon?"

"Maud says I broke three hearts, the way I left without a word. Hers, Olivia's, her mom's."

Bailey said softly, "Four."

"Don't you start. Please."

She nodded. "How does it feel to you now?"

"That I need to make amends. Not patch things up and start over. More like, I've been given this incredible chance to apologize the only way that matters. By doing better this time around." He hesitated, then added, "As far as I'm concerned, this is as close to a Christmas miracle as I've ever come."

She swung around so as to study him full on. "Have you worked out how that's happening with the lady in question?"

"Maybe. Olivia's home is probably gone. Hard to say exactly, but that's how it looked to me. So I've offered her the spare room in my grandparents' place. Soon as they clear the roads and restore power, I think we should move in. Give her a safe place to start over."

He half expected her to laugh at him. Two people who had once been madly in love, now living together under one roof. As friends. It was beyond crazy.

Instead, Bailey said, "Come have dinner with me tonight."

17

Dillon returned to the station in midafternoon. He spent half an hour with Maud, going through queries from the state auditor, helping her with the proper wording and correct numbers. Most of it was make-work, demands for more detail from a man who would have preferred to give them nothing. Maud finally rose from her desk and told him to sit and do it himself, which was what he had been after all along. Another two hours and the forms were completed, the questions answered, the petty demands met. Dillon showered and dressed in clean but severely wrinkled clothes, and was standing outside when Porter emerged from his office. "You seen Olivia?"

"I thought she was with you."

"She left a while back for Gleason's." He adjusted his hat, said, "I've got to get on home. If you see the lady, tell her however the pictures turn out, she's already done us a world of good."

"Will do."

Five minutes after the chief departed, Olivia entered the front lot.

She was smiling.

It was not like she had cast aside her shadows. They were stained deep in her being, they still fractured her gaze. All there for anyone who knew her well enough to peer beneath the surface. Just the same, her smile was a thing of beauty. Dillon said, "You remind me of a girl I once knew. I always thought her smile was meant for someone twice her size."

"I've been doing some very good work."

"I'm glad. Really, really glad. Porter basically said the same."

"He hasn't seen the photographs yet."

"It sounded like just having the session with you was important." He took a long moment, studying her in their narrow shelter from the rain, glad in a strange way they were here. Together. In this moment. "I have a date."

"Whoa, Dillon. Who put the tiger in your tank?"

"That would be Bailey."

"Bailey, as in Griff's . . ."

"Ex. Right. Her."

She turned and studied the dimming light. Dillon

was suddenly fearful he had done a bad thing. Stolen away the woman's momentary happiness. Then she said, "In our hardest moments, when I was far enough from you and us to think outside the cage, I wondered."

"I'm not sure how I feel about you calling what we had a cage."

"Two people fighting, no holds barred," she said, addressing the gentle mist. "What would you call it?"

He decided that was a good moment to stay silent.

"I wondered," she repeated. "Maybe Bailey was a better fit."

"I never thought that," he said.

"No?"

"Not for a single solitary instant."

"But here you are." She looked at him, the smile still there, but filled with the wisdom of ages. And the sorrow. "Dressed in your finest duds."

"Hoping the wrinkles will fall out before she shows up."

"Too late." Olivia pointed to the car pulling through the main gates. "Here she comes now."

"So you're okay with this."

"Better than okay." She surprised him anew, reaching up and encircling her arms around his neck. A quick embrace, a wave to the lady driving the SUV, then she reached for the door and said, "Have a wonderful time."

When Dillon slipped into the car, Bailey greeted him with, "What was that I just saw?"

He watched Olivia step through the rain-swept doors. "Just being friends."

Bailey's home occupied the nether region north of town. That was what her parents called it, back when they welcomed him as easily and warmly as they might a close relative. Her father was a physio and chiropractor working out of the local hospital's rehab unit. Bailey's mom was a Pilates and yoga instructor long before it became all the rage. Dillon considered them the sort of people who defined the best California had to offer. Easygoing, self-contained, stoic, unflappable, honest. They cared without gushing. They gave, expecting nothing in return. Being accepted into their home was a princely reward.

They were a tight couple, calm in their ways and deeply in love. What they thought of Bailey's choice in a mate, they never said. As best man Dillon had been seated at the head table, and though both dabbed at tears during the festivities, neither had a harsh word or warning, not then nor in all the preceding months after Bailey declared Griff was the one. Her lifetime partner.

The nether region was their name for homes dotting the northern headlands. There was no beach, just

cliffs and a few scraggly cattle who were gradually replaced by ever grander houses. Theirs was a sprawl-
ing ranch, cluttered and comfortable. Neither parent
held much interest in housekeeping. Their rear door
was always open to Dillon. Right up to the last few
weeks of his life in Miramar, sweating over his appli-
cations to grow university-style wings. They were the
ones who shared the desperate hope and fear. The
only ones.

They occupied a new home now, a smaller version
of the place Bailey claimed as her own, set against the
far fence and separated by a new stand of fast-growing
firs. Their neighborhood still had power, an illuminated
peninsula jutting from a rain-darkened land. Dillon
stopped by there first, and saw in the calm expressions a mirror into the good times. The ones too easily dismissed by a man fighting so hard to get away.

When he bade them goodnight and took the walk
back up toward the house, a dark-haired sprite stood
by the rear door. "You're Dillon and I'm Elena."

Which meant she was named after Griff's mother.
"Hi, Elena. It's a pleasure to meet you."

"That's because you don't know me." She spun on
her heel and danced through the door. "Just wait.
Mom says I grow on people like bed lice."

"I said no such thing!"

"You thought it. Tell me I'm wrong."

"You're wrong!"

"Ha." She danced back to Dillon. "This afternoon I heard Mom tell her best friend you were the lover she never had."

"Elena Elizabeth Long, I am going wring your neck!"

Dillon followed her through the glassed-in garden room and into the kitchen, where a crimson-faced Bailey said, "Now is the perfect time for you to take my car and drive off into the sunset."

"Too late," Elena said. "Sunset's over."

"Go watch television. Read a book. Do math. Enjoy your final days on earth." Bailey's hands stayed busy washing vegetables. "I actually don't know what to say."

Dillon thought it best to change the subject. "Your mom said to tell you she has fresh sourdough coming out of the oven."

"Elena, go get us a loaf."

"Hokey-pokey."

"Better still, ask them if you can move in until you turn thirty."

"She'll laugh in my face."

When the child departed, Dillon said, "She's so much like her father it makes my eyes burn."

"I know, right?"

Dillon watched the rain spatter against the glass door.

"Go ahead and ask." When Dillon remained silent, Bailey said it for him. "How could Griff walk away from raising this amazing child? He never said. But I think it's two things."

"He's the veritable Peter Pan," Dillon said, watching the empty yard. "He'd rather die than grow up."

"That's true, but it's only part of the whole story." Bailey set an iron skillet on the stove, added butter and olive oil. "I think Elena scares him. He can only take her in measured doses."

"Scared of what?"

Bailey started to speak, then shook her head and simply replied, "You'll see."

Dinner was a Spanish omelet with home fries, sourdough with honey for dessert. Their living-dining room was dominated by a Christmas tree minus lights. There were baubles, cute sections of ribbons tied in bows, a teddy bear with wings at its peak.

Elena said, "Mom was too lazy to unravel last year's knot of fairy lights."

"It wasn't funny the first time, and you've been going downhill ever since. Now tell him the truth."

"Boring." When Bailey shot her a mom-look, Elena's voice became robotic. "No Christmas lights because we need to keep from overloading the already strained electrical grid. This is Mayor Mom's way of setting a good example."

The meal became spiced by Elena's tale of her last trip to Cabo. Learning how to dive with tanks, apparently something her horrified mother only learned about this very moment. Spearing a tuna, eating sushi on the boat's rear deck. Both ladies easy and happy and sad over Dillon's absent friend.

As they cleaned up, Elena gave a mock sigh and said, "I suppose now is the time you'll be telling me to scamper."

"It's what you deserve," her mother replied. "Chained in your room until you turn thirty."

But Dillon said, "Don't go." When both mother and child showed surprise, he said, "It's been a long time since I was inside a happy family."

Bailey stopped in the process of loading the dishwasher and stared at her daughter. "You can stay."

"Mom . . ."

"It's okay," Bailey told her. "I'll behave."

"Behave, as in, not bawling your eyes out again?"

"Promise."

Dillon asked, "What exactly is going on here?"

"My sweet darling child wants to grow up too soon," Bailey said. "If she gets her wish, this spring she'll be leaving me and Miramar behind."

Dillon looked from one to the other. "You're moving to Cabo?"

Bailey laughed. Or tried to. "Not on your sweet

bippy. Go ahead, darling. Tell our guest about what else you did in Cabo."

"Daddy took me to the casino in his hotel."

"And gave her two hundred dollars in chips," Bailey added. "And let her play blackjack. At the grown-up table. Welcome to Mexico."

"This is for real?"

"Go ahead, my little innocent dumpling. Tell."

"Daddy taught me to count cards."

"This was Giff's idea of how to spend happy evenings playing father," Bailey said.

"It was interesting at first," Elena said. "But it got real boring real fast."

"Counting cards," Dillon said. "Boring."

"I won sixteen hundred dollars," Elena said. "That part wasn't boring."

"Her daddy was soooo proud," Bailey said.

"So . . . not Cabo." Dillon looked from one to the other. "Then . . ."

"Santa Barbara," Elena replied, watching her mother. "Mom, you promised."

Bailey heaved a great huge sigh. "I'm a mayor. Mayors can control their tear ducts. It's part of our training."

Dillon asked, "Will someone please tell me what's going on?"

"My daughter has her heart set on attending the state school for gifted children . . ."

"*Mom!*"

"I'm okay."

Dillon asked, "What does that mean, gifted?"

"When my angel with the fractured halo was four, she was seated inside the grocery trolley, you know what I mean, right?"

"Of course."

"Mom loves telling this story," Elena said. "It might almost be true."

"There she was, watching the clerk ring up my groceries. When the woman was done, this little child sings out the exact amount. *Before* the number appeared on the register."

"Whoa."

"Exactly."

Dillon said, "So you're a math whiz."

"I might become one," Elena replied. "Someday. If I can only work out the Everest of problems that is standing between me and the school . . . *Mom.*"

"Observe. This is me staying supportive and dry-eyed."

Elena gave a hugely exasperated sigh. "I have to submit this concept. Something that shows I can think outside the box. It's not enough that I know numbers. They are looking for . . ."

Dillon offered, "Originality."

"Of course not." She offered him the same sort of exasperation she'd shown her mother. "I'm *ten.*"

"They require her to show an ability to think, to reason, to explore," Bailey said. "Their exact words."

Dillon gave that the beat it deserved, then said, "I might be able to help with that."

Elena gave him a very womanly look. Out of the side of her eyes, tight, suspicious, timeless. "Oh really."

Dillon nodded. "Can I use your laptop?"

18

"I'm going to tell this backwards from the way I learned," Dillon started. He had been worried that the years had faded his recollections. But soon as he started coding in the mathematical structure, it all came flooding back. "First about the man, then about his discovery. Is that okay?"

"I guess." Elena drew out the words, watching her mom more than Dillon.

"The man's name was Benoit Mandelbrot, and he was born in Warsaw. His father traded in used clothing. When he was eleven, his family sought a better life and emigrated to Germany. But Mandelbrot was Jewish, and they arrived just as the Nazis were coming to power. So off they went again, nearly penniless this time, trekking by foot across two countries, and winding up in the French town of Tulle. They went for the simple reason that a friend was willing to help them settle. This friend was a rabbi, and a teacher, and during the war years he helped spark Mandelbrot's love of math."

The memories were fired by the light in Elena's gaze. The hunger so similar to his own early years, how he found refuge in studying about a man who had endured far worse than himself. And triumphed. "Mandelbrot rose from nothing to become the head of IBM Computers."

"For real?"

"Not just that, but he served as professor first at Harvard and then Yale. And he held honorary positions in France's top scientific institute."

"I've never heard of him."

"He invented the term *fractal*. Have you ever heard of that?"

The young girl frowned. "Somewhere."

"Mandelbrot had his time of fame back before I was born. And for math geeks it was the wrong kind of fame. His concepts got taken up by the yoga crowd."

"Who?"

"That's what I called them. Latter-day hippies, though by then the term had gone out of fashion."

"Okay, now you've totally lost me."

"Doesn't matter. What's important is, the math geeks took his work, basically stole the core concepts, worked on it, added their names to the process, then moved on."

She waited a long moment, then asked what Dillon had hoped to hear. "So how does this help me?"

"Because this guy's work, what he discovered, it's *everywhere*. The Mandelbrot set is used in weather patterning. Hydrology. Neurology. Linguistics. Software design. Computer graphics. On and on." Dillon tapped the screen. "But the core concept, what drove all this, has basically been sidelined. No one is looking at the pure math that underlies all this. The math geeks—"

"Why do you call them that?"

Dillon acknowledged the question with a nod. "Jealousy, mostly. I wish I had their ability. *Your* ability. I don't. I'm just an accountant."

Bailey spoke for the first time. "There is no *just*."

"It's true."

"Don't downplay your own gifts," Bailey said. "Mayor's orders."

Elena said, "She gets like that sometimes."

"Anyway, the people looking at Mandelbrot's work nowadays are engineers. Technicians. They *apply*. But the sheer potential, what else might be uncovered from the basic structure, that's lost to the history books. Toward the end of his life, Mandelbrot talked and wrote about how we had only touched the surface of what could be discovered." He pointed to the darkened screen. "Mandelbrot's formula showed how visual complexity can be created from very simple rules. Okay, simple for people like you. Things that we class as chaotic or messy, such as clouds or shorelines or financial markets or even the structure of leaves, actually have a very defined sense of order. If only we look at them the right way."

Dillon drew up the first pattern. "This is an online sample of a Mandelbrot set."

Bailey settled on the couch next to her daughter. "Scooch over."

Elena pressed herself in tight next to Dillon. "That is so totally awesome."

"This is nothing. Watch." Dillon selected an edge of the design, and magnified. "No matter how much you zoom in on any point in the structure, you get smaller and smaller patterns of the exact same design. Mandelbrot called this concept fractal geometry, and to his dying breath insisted it was the core element that defined all of nature."

He felt Elena release the tension in her body, take a long slow breath, and announce, "This could definitely work."

"I'm glad you think so."

Bailey said, "And now is the time when you say *thank you*."

Elena nodded slowly. "Chills."

Dillon smiled over the child's head, loving how close he felt to her mother. "You're welcome."

19

An hour or so later, Bailey signaled it was time. As Dillon rose from the sofa, she asked her daughter, "You'll be okay while I take our guest back?"

Elena told Dillon, "I learned the meaning of *rhetorical* early on. Part of bringing up Mom."

Dillon told her mother, "This young lady can be scary."

"You have no idea." Bailey kissed the top of her daughter's head. "Be good."

"I assume this means I'm not welcome to come along for the ride?"

"Oh, I think we've had enough of your lip for one night. You know what to do if you need anything, correct?"

"Grab the speargun from the back of my closet. Load, aim, shoot."

"Elena."

"Go find Grandad." Then she surprised them both.

Elena rose from the couch, stood on tiptoes, gestured for Dillon to lean over, and wrapped her arms around his neck. "Please come again. Please."

"I would like nothing better."

She branded his cheek with a kiss, then released him and stepped back. "Is it true what Mom said, you're living in the jail?"

Dillon followed Bailey toward the kitchen door. "I have a cell all my very own."

"Welcome to my world."

Bailey did not even turn around. "Elena!"

"Sorry. It just slipped out." She blew Dillon a second kiss. "Tell Mom, for once I approve."

Bailey did not speak until they were backing out of the drive. "I actually don't know what to say."

Dillon did not have that problem. "Your daughter is truly amazing."

She did not respond until they were on the main road heading back toward town. Her voice was mildly fractured when she said, "I also don't know what I'm going to do without her."

Dillon saw the damp glistening on her cheeks and decided now was an excellent time to change the subject. "Can I ask a favor? There's a house on the road leading to our valley road. A ton of Christmas ornaments in the front yard, all dark. And the windows—"

"The Inghams' place. With all the candles." Bailey took the next left. "Absolutely."

They did not speak again until they were parked
outside the home. Dillon saw four other vehicles sitting there, with more driving slowly past. If anything,
there were more candles tonight. Dozens and dozens
of glimmering flames, defying the dark and the storm.
Bailey said exactly what Dillon was thinking. "I
know it sounds crazy. But this gives me hope."

He nodded. Silent. Thinking.

"Thad Ingham works for the fire service. He told
me they wake up most mornings to find boxes of candles stacked on his doorstep and lining the entry to
his garage. His kids think it's the angels' way of saying they're doing something good."

They remained there a long moment, then Bailey
restarted her car, turned back toward town, and said,
"So tell me about Olivia."

Dillon looked at her. "Excuse me?"

"I have a dear friend who wants to talk with Olivia
about something important. He needs to know
what's her state of mind." Bailey met his gaze. "I'm
not for one instant pretending there's no personal interest in the matter."

The direct and honest Bailey Long. The childhood
friend all grown up and still holding on to the things
he had valued most. Despite everything. "It seems to
me there are two Olivias. The one who was put through

an awful time in LA. And arrived here pretty close to crushed." He pointed to the curb. "Pull over, will you? I don't like how you're driving with both eyes not on the road."

"You've never been a mother." Just the same, she turned her attention to the way ahead. "And the other Olivia?"

"A very gifted artist with her camera," Dillon replied. "I have the impression she's actually coming into her own."

"Meaning what, exactly?"

"Her jobs in LA were at least partly the result of her husband—"

"Ex-husband. Speaking for all women everywhere, there has never been a more important prefix since the discovery of language."

"May I continue?"

"Look. You're talking to the mayor. I'm required by law to correct men who don't know how to say what they mean."

Dillon started to reply that he now understood what Elena had been talking about. But the trace of past tears was still there on Bailey's cheeks, so he merely asked, "You've seen Olivia's portrait of the family?"

"The one in Gleason's window." Bailey nodded. "The whole town is talking. Far as I'm concerned, it ranks up there with the candles in the hope department."

"Tell her that, okay? Olivia needs to hear it. Especially coming from you."

"Duly noted. Back to my question."

"Whatever comes from her photography here in Miramar, it's all due to her talent. This is her chance to fly solo. If she's successful, it's because she made it happen."

Bailey passed the town's main supermarket, drove down rain-slick streets, and finally responded. "It seems to me the same might be said about you. The Dillon who arrived here with his own hard-luck tale. And the guy who is doing his best to save our town from bankruptcy."

He nodded. "I've been thinking about that."

"And?"

"My grandmother used to say Miramar was a town made for second chances."

"All you had to do was move beyond the past, and grab hold of the hour when it came," Bailey agreed. "I've heard that all my life."

But Dillon was still caught by those earlier times. "My grandmother learned never to say that in front of my dad. He'd start shouting and throwing things. Then toke on his bowl and snarl at the world until he passed out."

Bailey waited until she approached a stop sign to turn and say, "That was another time. The Dillon here beside me is all grown up. There are all sorts of second chances just waiting to pounce."

The car remained silent until Bailey pulled through the police station's main gates. She parked, turned off the engine, and said, "Back to the personal angle I've been dancing around."

Dillon did not pretend to be in the dark. "Me and Olivia."

She slid around, tucked one knee on the central console, faced him squarely. "And?"

"Friends to the end."

"As in, friends with benefits?"

Which was just like the Bailey he'd grown up liking so very, very much. "If that chance arrives, and I don't think it will. But if it does, I hope the ghosts of Christmas past will be enough to warn me off." He gave her a chance to respond, then asked, "Will you tell me what this thing is, concerning her? I mean, you know, other than the obvious."

"It's best if she hears it first."

Dillon nodded. "Thank you for a lovely evening."

"I was just thinking the very same thing."

"Please tell your daughter I can still feel her kiss on my cheek."

Bailey's eyes gleamed copper-dark as she reached

over and placed her hand on the exact same spot. "You'll remember what I said earlier."

"About chances," Dillon replied. "And not pouncing if a certain door creaks open."

She released him, settled behind the wheel, and restarted the car. "You bet your bippy."

20

The next morning, Dillon woke to find three sticky notes attached to his blanket and a fourth, amazingly, dangling from his forehead.

Maud: *Arnaud had a delivery of eggs, cheese and soft tortillas. If you move fast enough he's offering breakfast burritos while they last. Go to the diner's rear door.*

And a second from Maud: *Go straight from the diner to the fire station. Look for the fire chief begging on the street out front. He's collecting pennies for a new ER vehicle. See if you can help.*

Bailey: *Thanks for last night. Ditto from Elena. We need to talk about feds and shifting timelines. They're opening their wallets tomorrow. PS, You need to do something about that bear hibernating in your cell.*

And finally, this from Olivia: *Eleven o'clock. Here. Urgent. Help.*

*   *   *

When Dillon entered the station, Olivia was nowhere to be found. He smiled at how everyone
present wished him a good morning. Even Maud. A
first.

Dillon left the station, walked the windswept four
blocks, and found about a dozen locals standing by
the diner's rear door, squatting on the pavement,
seated on a ratty picnic table used by the staff on break.
They were a motley West Coast mélange of races and
professions—hospital staff, fire crew, construction
workers, a cop, and a tuna boat skipper with two
deckhands. Dillon greeted several that he recognized.
He accepted two burritos and a large coffee, insisted
on paying, then bid the crew farewell and headed out.
He ate as he walked. He had forgotten how good it
felt to be on the clock. A busy day crammed with
work that held real meaning. And something more.
This was Miramar. The hometown he had fled in
frantic desperation. Welcoming him back with a need
he was born to fill.

The fire station was down the same side street as
the town hall and anchored an entire block. Which
was good, because all the fire engines and crew's personal vehicles and three EMT vehicles were all jammed
into the vacant lot next to the actual station. The lot

itself was graded and graveled, which meant they did not plow giant tire-size furrows in the earth every time there was a call-out.

All three of the station's bay doors were pulled up, revealing any number of people scurrying about. The only difference between the fire crew and the volunteers was, the crewmembers wore matching boots and coveralls. The interior was jammed with toys, clothes, personal items, candy—on and on the stacks went, lining the walls and forming colorful mountains where the vehicles should have resided. Volunteers in Santa hats staffed two long tables, filling sacks and wrapping presents. While Dillon watched, a pickup pulled up, beeped its horn, and four of the crew hurried out. They unloaded the rear hold while Chief Hurst chatted with the driver. Then it was the turn of volunteers working the tables. Soon as the cargo bed was emptied, others began carrying out sacks and gifts.

Charlie shook hands with the driver, then sauntered over to Dillon and said, "Back in the late fire season, we served as a focal point for donations. When these storms started piling in off the Pacific, all the churches and other volunteer groups went back to using our station as the staging area." He pointed toward the town hall. "There's another crew working in the community center, keeping lists up-to-date, watching for the folks who can't get out, handling the high-value items like electronics. We gather and sort everything else."

A faint whisper of an idea began forming, but Dillon could not make out more than a niggling sense that he was missing something important. He stayed silent, trying to figure out . . .

Charlie Hurst went on. "The good news is, we haven't had an actual call-out since forever. The town is too wet to burn. Which means my crew serve as emergency backup to everybody else. Except Porter. I volunteered. Twice. Porter said the idea of deputizing my bunch and loaning them guns gives him nightmares."

The chief gave him a quick tour of the vehicles, pointing out the storm's damage to several, the general weary state of others. They entered the station by way of a side door. Charlie said, "Welcome to the hurricane's eye."

In odd contrast to the efficient, orderly, and smooth-running station, the fire chief's office was a dismal wreck. Piles of unopened letters marked OVERDUE, receipts, catalogues, half-finished fire reports, all jumbled into a tsunami-size mess dominating every flat surface.

Charlie did not even try for a defense. "I guess I let things slip a little."

"The fire service doesn't have an accountant?"

"In theory." He lifted the mess off his chair, searched for a place to set it down, then dropped it on the floor next to a pair of muddy boots. "We share the town's bookkeeper. What's a polite way to say the lady is a waste of space?"

"No idea."

"Last spring she came down with something the doc hasn't been able to name. Been on sick leave ever since. Tell the truth, she was struggling long before then. Her mother is on the town council and a close personal friend of Bailey's late mom. Two weeks ago, Mayor Bailey finally shut that door."

Dillon read the unspoken, in the way Charlie refused to meet his gaze. "They want me to take charge?"

Charlie turned furtive. "Don't tell anybody I spoke out of turn. Bailey would brand my sorry hide."

"Tell the truth, I appreciate the heads-up. It's nice having a chance to think things over."

"You and I are going to get along just fine." Charlie led him back through the station, introduced a few of his crew, brought him back outside. When they were standing by the side alcove, staring over the weary engines, he asked, "How hard can we milk the feds' cow?"

"I need a specific for instance."

Charlie pointed at the crowded lot. "Can I build us a new station?"

"I haven't read all the fine print. But my guess is, that would be a dollar or two over the line."

He dropped his hand. "How about a Christmas bonus for the crew?"

"Nix on the bonus. That's actually in the statutes."

"You're kidding, right?"

"I could read you the clause. It's loaded with wherefores and with-alls. Put you right to sleep."

"Send me screaming from the station, more like." He squinted at the open bay doors. "So, nix on the bonus. Shame. They deserve it."

"What we can do is put them in for hazard pay." Dillon loved how the chief brightened. He cautioned, "We need to be totally clear how your budget can't cover that."

"No problem."

"That's the key issue to opening the feds' spigot," Dillon went on. "Show you've run through your annual budget. Give them evidence the emergency has broken the bank."

"Which it has."

"In that case, my job is simple. I just need to put the numbers in the right boxes and write it all up using the proper federal-speak. These guys never met a wherefore they didn't like."

"You call that simple?"

"Whiz-o-bang-o, the money flows. I hope."

"You and me both." The furtive jerky gaze returned. "So, are you taking the job?"

Dillon loved having a reason to grin. "What job would that be?"

21

Olivia and Gleason decided on one black-and-white photograph of Porter with his family, and a color print of their daughter. Both were to be printed on the textured cotton sheets of paper, which hopefully would add to the portrait feel. The previous evening they had debated the choices, then fiddled with shading and color and illumination. That morning they continued the good-natured debate for another hour or so. Neither of them were in any hurry. Now and then Gleason left her alone in the back while he tended to a customer's needs. The solitary moments granted her a chance to release the occasional shiver of pure joy.

She was late for her meeting with the mayor before both were printed and approved and rolled into separate tubes. Olivia hugged the older man, thanked him profusely, smiled over his grouchy embarrassment, kissed his cheek, and fled. She rushed up the main street, flying really. She loved the feel of cool rain falling on her face. She relished the sensation of being surrounded by a town that had welcomed her back, despite everything. She was moved nearly to tears by the stoic determination she found on so many faces, the California spirit coming out strong as summer sunlight. They would endure, rebuild, move on. Her feet scarcely touched the damp sidewalk, or so it felt.

Not even her certainty over why Bailey had requested this meeting could dampen her mood. The mayor's note had been waiting when Olivia emerged from her cell that morning. It had simply requested they meet with Berto Acosta, and had given a time.

That had been enough.

Berto Acosta was Miramar's builder of choice. At least, he was for those who could afford him. And who put up with Berto's rigid stance on design. He refused to build what he classed as LA-style tin-pot palaces. Berto used the finest materials, constructed to the highest codes, and charged accordingly.

Berto's wife Emelia was also head of the town council.

The builder had twice made the journey south, meeting with Olivia in LA. This after numerous letters and phone calls, both to Olivia and her mother, asking to buy their home. The reason was simple. Their cottage sat on a three-acre plot of land, with a grand view over the town and the coast beyond. Second in size only to Dillon's property. Who also refused to give Costa the time of day.

But things were different now. The cottage where she had grown up was no longer habitable. And Olivia needed the money.

Which was why she had begged Dillon to come to her rescue. Because this was one conversation she could not handle by herself.

Soon as Olivia opened the station door, the mayor rounded on her. Bailey possessed a remarkable bark for such a slender waif. "Finally! Hasn't anybody ever told you it's a fineable offence, keeping your elected officials pacing the floor?"

Maud did not look up from her computer. "Bailey only got here two minutes ago."

"Two long minutes! And that's not important. Everybody should be here and ready to stand and salute when the mayor . . ." Bailey was halted mid-sentence by how Olivia ignored her. "Are you even listening?"

"Porter, could you step over here?" She set her two cardboard tubes on Dillon's orderly desk, popped the top off one, then hesitated.

The moment deserved some fine words, a mention of how grateful she was for all this group had done for her, whatever. But her mind remained an excited blank. So she simply unfurled the print and held it with both arms extended.

The silence that greeted her portrait was perhaps the nicest response she had ever received. Oh, there had been some lovely moments with stars as well. They started out cautious, cynical, playing the role, fearful of what she might do with their off-stage image. Gradually, with extreme caution, they had come to trust her. Olivia had loved her ability to surprise.

But this was something else entirely.

Porter finally declared, "That's not me."

"Oh, it's you, all right," Maud said.

"It's who you don't like to think the world can see," Bailey agreed. "But we know it's there."

"Hidden deep," Maud agreed. "Miles down, most of the time."

"But it's there." Bailey smiled at Olivia. "This is amazing."

Suddenly they were all talking at once. Asking how she managed to get the light just so. And weren't the women incredible, how mother and daughter were mirror images a generation apart. And wanting her to do them, their families, friends, whatever. Olivia let them gabble on for a time, then said, "There's one more."

She anchored the first print on Dillon's desk, using his closed laptop and a stapler and pen-holder to keep the print flat. Then she opened the second tube and unfurled the print.

Celia shone with a sad luminescence, the joy of youth balanced by the sorrow of coming departure.

The colt's head formed a perfect counterpoint to the young woman's beauty. One hand stroked the forelock, but her attention was captured by something beyond the camera's reach. Her smile was timeless.

The look on Porter's face said it all.

Olivia said softly, "Merry Christmas."

Porter went through the motions of a shift change, assigning duties in a subdued voice, initialing documents Maud held for him, having a quiet word with the mayor. All the while, he kept circling back to Dillon's desk. Studying the two portraits spread over the surface. Olivia remained by the side wall, feeling isolated even when others spoke to her. There was a timeless quality to the moment. As if she had managed to step outside the flow of hours and chatter and people. And could stand there in this wonderful solitude, filled with an inner glow over a job well done.

Dillon's response was interesting. He studied the two photographs in silence, holding to a faint smile, nodding to something that remained unspoken. Olivia had the distinct impression her work confirmed a secret he had not shared, at least with her. But as she started to ask what he was thinking, Porter walked up. The chief wore police rain gear, which seemed to double his girth.

"I keep hoping the words are going to come to me," Porter said. "Find some way to say what I'm thinking."

"It's okay. Really."

He nodded and fumbled with his cap. "This will go a long way to healing our Christmas."

"I'm glad." She touched the border of their daughter's portrait. "If you like, I can go ahead and have these framed."

"That would be great. You just do what you think works best." He touched the same point where her own fingers had been. "I'm not going to talk payment. Not now."

Olivia wished there was a way to make them a gift. A gesture of thanks for all he had done to ease her reentry. If only. In the end, she just nodded.

Dillon waited for the chief to depart, then told her, "Time for round two."

As soon as she and Dillon entered the chief's office, Bailey started before the door was even shut. "I have been placed in an enormously uncomfortable situation."

"You already said that," Olivia pointed out.

"When was that?"

"This morning. When you asked for this meeting."

"Well, it's true." She stepped to Porter's desk, re-arranged a couple of items, stepped away. "Berto's wife is head of the town council and effectively my boss. At least on paper. She is also my biggest advocate. I've never needed her help more than now. This is the first time she's ever asked me for anything."

Olivia offered Dillon a slow and emphatic nod. He smiled in understanding, and took the lead. "It's okay."

"I was addressing Olivia."

Olivia replied, "Dillon speaks for me today."

The mayor protested, "Olivia . . ."

"That's how it needs to be."

Bailey pondered the floor by her feet. "This just keeps getting worse by the minute."

Dillon drew four chairs into the center of the room. "Bailey, please come sit down."

"No."

"We know what Berto wants. This conversation is happening at the right time." Dillon waited until both women were seated, then continued. "Berto has been after me as well. He can't make it happen like he wants unless . . ." Dillon spotted the builder through the door's glass panel. "Here he comes now."

For such a big man, Berto Acosta carried himself with remarkable grace. His gestures were measured, his voice gentle, his expression sincere. This was a gentleman accustomed to discussing multimillion-dollar homes with people who could afford them. But he was also a builder, with hands large as skillets and a manner that demanded respect.

Soon as Berto was seated, he began almost the identical spiel to what Olivia had heard in LA. Berto sketched out his idea for Olivia's nearly three-acre property. Four buildings of three stories each, two condos per floor, a total of twenty-four residences framed by sculpted gardens, pool, gym, underground parking. The longer he spoke, the more excited he became. He paused then, and his expression turned somber. "Have you visited your former home?"

Dillon spoke for the first time. "Let's set that aside for the moment."

Acosta showed a theatrical surprise, as if he had not noticed Dillon's presence until that moment. "And who exactly am I addressing?"

Olivia replied, "Dillon speaks for me."

"Does he." Berto straightened in his chair. He did not appear the least bit upset. Instead, there was a new light in his dark gaze. A spark of heightened interest. He told Dillon, "Your grandfather was the finest stonemason and bricklayer I ever met."

"And you were the only builder who could bring him out of retirement," Dillon said.

"That's right. I did."

"Twice," Dillon added.

Berto smiled. "Can't say I ever learned to appreciate his wine."

"Did you drink it?"

"Not unless he was watching me." He straightened the crease to his trousers. "You were in banking, yes?"

"Close. Securities and investment."

"Of course. Your grandmother told me."

"When you pitched your development project to my grandparents."

Another smile, the motion almost theatrical. "I did indeed."

"Twice."

"Actually, it was three times," Berto replied. "But who's counting."

Dillon continued, "Let's say we agree."

Berto's response was to go completely still.

"What if we both say yes," Dillon repeated. "Now. Today."

"Both of you?"

"We're talking hypothetical at this point," Dillon replied. "But yes. All nine and a half acres."

"But . . . Your grandfather swore I'd never build on his land."

"That's right. He did. But my grandmother thought your plan was a good one. And the last time I came home, she gave me her blessing to do with the land as I saw fit. Once they were both gone. Which they are."

The builder opened his mouth, but no sound came.

"A combined property totaling nine and a half acres," Dillon repeated. "Zoned for multiple-family construction because you made it happen."

The chair squeaked a mild protest as Berto straightened. "You've obviously come with something in mind."

"That's right. I have."

Berto was all business. "Why don't you go ahead and lay it out."

"Joined together you have the largest elevated plot in the central coast zoned for multiple families. That has to be worth—"

"It is my turn to interrupt," Berto said. "Your pitch is unnecessary. I know the potential."

"Extend my grandad's retainer wall to protect Olivia's acreage from any future storm," Dillon went on, calm as ever. "Level the vineyard, and you're ready to build."

"I'm waiting."

Olivia's sense of distance remained with her still. She was able to view their discussion not as a pending loss, but rather as a fencing match. The two men knew their positions and their steps. They circled and watched and prepared. And despite the fact they were discussing the final demolition of her childhood home, Olivia's calm was maintained.

The change in Dillon was so sharply focused here, Olivia felt as if she could almost photograph the man's invisible elements. The Dillon she knew in their early years certainly had the sort of cooly gentle streak she saw on display now. But his view of life was mostly shaped by a constant conflict with the world around him. The younger Dillon had met every day with a latent rage, a burning frustration with the cage that held him. And the young Olivia had known how to release that fury. The memory burned her now, watching Dillon fence with the builder. Her ability to manipulate him into fury had held an almost sexual appeal. At times she had even enjoyed it. Because Dillon had raged for her.

"Two penthouse apartments," Dillon said. "One for each of us. Which I'm guessing will be more or less the value of that land in its current state."

Berto offered a thoughtful, "That is certainly worth considering."

Bailey shifted uncomfortably in her chair. "Maybe I should go."

"Please stay," Dillon said. "I need your help."

"What possible good could I do with your trading land for two condos?"

"I'm not done," Dillon replied.

"Here we go," Berto said.

When Dillon was certain Bailey would remain, he told the builder, "Three more things. No hidden agenda. First, we're broke. Both of us need help covering our living expenses."

"You're thinking . . ."

"A twenty thousand dollar signing bonus," he replied. "Each. Ten thousand dollars more at the start of each six month period, until the condos are finished. Each."

Berto gave that a longish pause, then replied, "I'm not walking out just yet."

"Next, we don't have any place to live. Do you have an empty show-home or condo? Two bedrooms, two offices."

"Still sitting," Berto replied. "I assume you've saved the worst for last."

"Definitely not the worst," Dillon replied, and offered the morning's first smile. "But maybe the craziest."

The longer Olivia's sense of distance remained in place, the more she was able to separate herself into two components. On the one hand, she listened as Dillon outlined a concept that ignited a genuine sense of excitement in both Bailey and Acosta.

On the other, she was granted an opportunity to view herself. In safety and calm. Despite everything.

She had arrived in Miramar burdened by a sense of defeat. The life she had built for herself was over. She was forced to return empty-handed to the world she had struggled so hard to leave behind. Her sense of shame was just another component of a life gone wrong.

And yet.

For the first time in months, Olivia felt herself utterly freed from all the burdens she had been carrying. Dillon's remarkable plan, the way these two locals almost shouted their agreement and ideas, all formed components of a new day.

Dillon addressed her directly then. "You're so quiet."

"Listening," she replied. "Thinking."

Bailey asked, "But you're okay with this?"

"I am." Even her voice sounded removed from the room and their growing enthusiasm. "Yes."

"Are you sure about that?" The man she had once wanted to love forever leaned in close. "Olivia, we don't want to push you into anything you're not—"

She halted him with an upraised hand. She told the three of them, "This is a true Christmas gift."

22

Berto Acosta stepped into the station's front room, his demeanor almost jolly. Any hint of reserve he might have felt over Dillon's terms was lost to the anticipation of putting things into motion. Bailey called the fire chief, then told Dillon to hurry on over to the station, as Charlie Hurst was there and waiting.

Olivia watched.

When it was just the two of them, Bailey showed no interest in setting her own day into motion. Instead, she said, "Dillon's idea is a good one."

"It's better than that," Olivia replied. "It brings together strands of my life and my past that . . ."

"What?"

She took a long breath. "I arrived back thinking my future was in grave peril. If I had any future at all."

Bailey tilted her head to one side, as if needing to

inspect Olivia from a different angle. "You don't mind losing your home?"

Olivia shook her head. "The day after I arrived, Dillon took me up there."

"In Porter's pickup. I heard."

"I couldn't go in."

Bailey nodded. "The damage."

"No. Well, yes, I suppose, in a way. But it was mostly the memories. They crowded me out."

"Terrible thing, memories," Bailey said. "And all the regret they carry."

"That too."

"And now?"

Olivia felt time slow. There in Bailey's gaze was a glint of something new. Fear, perhaps. Tension. And . . .

With a start, Olivia understood.

Bailey was in love. With Dillon Farrow. The man Olivia once claimed as her very own.

The realization lanced her, such that Olivia drew in a sharp breath. It was crazy, thinking she could read the other woman's mind. And yet, what she most felt was a burning sense of release.

Moving forward.

Olivia replied, "My mother would be absolutely beside herself with joy over Dillon's plan."

"Really?"

Olivia nodded slowly. Not so much in agreement as knowing that if it was going to be said, she would have to do the saying. "Dillon is a wonderful man."

Her statement was enough to reveal the woman's nerves. "And you two . . ."

"We have turned the page." Olivia gave each word a quiet emphasis. "Dillon and I are friends for life. And that's all. Who we were, what we meant to each other, that is finished." She started to add, *and almost finished us in the process.* But there would be other times to relive the battles and the sparks and the shame it all now caused. So she simply said, "We were different people then. For better or worse, we've changed."

Bailey tasted several responses before asking, "Is he really who he appears to be?"

Olivia did not pretend at misunderstanding. "Dillon has gone through the fire. No question." It was her turn to stare at the empty doorway. "The events that brought him back here also broke him, at least partly. But so far all I can see . . ."

A whispered, "Tell me."

"The rage that powered him forward is gone. I'm not sure what fills that void in his life, or whether the anger and frustration and desire for battle will ever return. There's no way of knowing." She felt her eyes burn at the memories. And the regret. She swallowed hard, pushed it all back, crammed it down tight inside. Breathed. And went on, "He always had a gentle streak. Now that's all I see in him. The tenderness he's shown me, the way he's looked out for what I need, what's best . . ."

Olivia had to stop there. Gather herself. She had said more than enough.

"It scares me to death," Bailey said. "This thing has hit me like a tsunami."

Olivia wiped her face. Nodded.

"And my daughter," Bailey went on. "Elena has never, not once in her entire life, talked about somebody the way she does about Dillon."

A sudden cloud of regret almost swamped her. Seeing how Bailey's face was effused with a hope strong as daylight. Remembering days when she was the one who felt . . .

Olivia knew a moment's keening desire for a different outcome. Where they had handled things better, done things differently. Made the moment theirs to share, rather than this. Seeing a new love bloom in a good woman, and know it was time for her to move on.

It was the most natural thing in the world to rise and walk over and gather the mayor up in an embrace. Olivia said it then. Whispered, really. No volume was necessary between friends. "Go for it."

23

Dillon stopped in the station's front room for a time, mostly because it was the polite thing to do. He listened to Berto and the others begin to fill in his idea and give it a more concrete form. But nothing they discussed required his input. When he started for the exit, Berto asked, "Going somewhere?"

"I thought I'd try and get a start on the fire chief's records."

"Good luck with that," Porter said. He watched Bailey enter the station texting on her phone. "I'm pretty sure that mess is what drove our former book-keeper around the bend."

"That poor soul had a serious case of the crazies from day one," Maud offered. "Charlie's idea of records only nudged her a trifle in that direction."

Berto took that as his cue. "I better grab my crew and take a look at a cottage that needs shifting."

"Correction." Bailey pocketed her phone. "You're

going to pace around your new property while your crew does all the real work."

"Thinking and planning are real jobs," Berto protested.

"Oh, sure." Maud pointed to the builder's considerable gut. "Look at all the muscle you're building."

Dillon followed the builder from the station, refused his offer of a lift, and enjoyed the walk through town. He felt as if the gray season had gifted him a different set of eyes. He viewed Miramar without any of the frustrated rage that had propelled him out. Gone too was the bitter regret that had brought him back. In its place was . . .

As Dillon entered the fire chief's office, he decided there was no way to describe how he felt just then. *Different* was the only word that came to mind.

The mess blanketing the fire chief's desk looked even worse than the day before. If that was even possible.

As he seated himself and began the sorting process, Dillon found himself recalling other afternoons, other places. Losing himself in numbers and analysis, making sense of an impossible market, thriving on how others trusted him to get it right.

And look where it took them. Straight off the financial cliff. All his clients and partners, not just burned by the markets. They were incinerated. Because he failed to see the assassins lurking behind his numbers . . .

"Whose dog just died?"

Dillon jerked so hard he spilled papers all over the floor. "Elena. Hi."

"Don't hi me." Bailey's daughter closed the office door. "What's the matter? And don't tell me nothing. I get enough of those nothings from Mom."

"You sound so much like your mother. Not the voice. It's how you see below the surface."

"Is that a very adult attempt to change the subject?"

"Sort of."

"Nice try." Elena pulled over a chair, seated herself, then asked more softly, "What's wrong?"

"You pulled me away from some very hard memories."

"Terrible things. Or so I'm told. I'm supposedly too young to have any."

"I don't believe that for a second."

She bounced the chair a couple of times. "Change the subject?"

"In a heartbeat."

"What are you doing, and can I help?"

"Aren't you supposed to be using the Christmas break to, you know . . ."

"Moon over some boy band? Call my bestie and giggle about some teenage version of dear old Dad?"

"I was actually thinking about your application."

"Oh. That." She waved it aside. Which again shot him back to earlier days, and how Bailey could verbally fence her way out of any tight spot. "Shall we now return to the question you're not answering?"

Dillon felt intimately connected to Elena's mother. Glimpsing what Bailey probably saw every day, her daughter captured in that incredibly brief moment between child and woman. "I'm supposed to prepare a major ask for the feds. Miramar wants Washington to pay for structural rebuilds and replace some damaged equipment. We're talking sums approaching outer orbit."

"So, can I volunteer a few boringly idle hours?"

"Absolutely." Dillon shifted over enough to let Elena move in beside him. "I would pay you, if I had the money."

He sketched out what he needed her to do, sorting and collating items that were tied to loaned equipment. Dillon found a distinct comfort in working alongside this brilliant young woman. He fielded a few questions, then when silence reigned he again lost himself in puzzling out what the feds needed. When he was ready, Dillon began filling in the massive forms.

Sometime later, he straightened, stretched, and discovered Elena was watching him. Her gaze was solemn, her expression almost sad. "What's the matter?"

"You know how equations are split into two basic elements." It was not a question.

Dillon had no idea how to respond. This woman-child looked ready to weep, but she was talking about math. He shut the laptop and swiveled around so as to face her. And waited.

"Even the most complex equation can be broken down into definable parts. Constants, terms, operator. I'm not telling you anything you don't already know, right?"

Dillon remained silent. Motionless.

"One-step equations. That was my second true love. Mom being the first. Dad too, but Daddy . . ." Something about speaking about Dillon's former best friend caused Elena to stop and wipe her face. "I don't even remember when my love of math really took hold. Mom says I was four. At least, that's when she first saw me trying to copy out equations from a program on educational TV."

Dillon forced himself to breathe. Waited.

"What I do remember is how amazing it felt. One set of symbols or numbers, connected by operators. Add, subtract, multiply, square roots, whatever. And then the equal sign. And on the other side of that sign . . ." Another impatient swipe at tears. "The outcome was truth. That's how I saw it. A question on the left, a truth on the right. Before, mystery. After, something new. Something awesome."

It seemed the most natural thing in the world to reach over and take her hand. Elena's fingers were still damp from her tears.

When Elena looked down, the motion was enough to release another tear. As it landed on the back of Dillon's hand, he feared his heart would break without understanding why.

"People are so different. The math doesn't work out. The answers aren't there." She spoke to his hand now. "But the before and after is still very clear. The before, Mom was alone and it hurt her. The after, she meets you. But what is waiting for her on the other side of this equation? I can't figure out . . ."

Dillon remained silent.

"She doesn't see how it's already moved to the other side of the equation. The transition is real and it's happened. For me too. I know it has, and I can't help it." A hard swallow, another dislodged tear. "I don't know who's more scared, me or Mom."

Dillon gave it as long as he could manage, then asked, "Would it be okay if I hugged you?"

She did not raise her head. "I think I would like that more than just about anything."

Dillon had no experience when it came to hugging a girl this age. When Elena's slender form slipped into his arms, he felt his heart expand. Like he had been waiting for this moment, yearning for this chance. Which was impossible, of course. But still.

And then the mother walked in.

Dillon's mind went from utterly content to full-on panic. He wanted to step back, say something, do anything to defuse what might have been a major wrong move. But his arms refused to unlock, and his mind remained a frantic blank. So he just stood there, trapped in his own version of the deer in headlights, when . . .

Bailey gave the two of them a purely feminine smile, then asked, "Is there room for one more?"

Elena shifted a fraction to her left and released half her hold on Dillon. While her face remained pressed firmly to his chest, she waved her right fingers in Mayor Mom's general direction.

"Oh goodie." Bailey shifted forward and melted into position, holding them both with surprising strength.

Dillon felt the pair take a long, unified breath. In. Out.

Bailey murmured, "I needed this. Sooo much."

Elena rubbed her face against Dillon's shirt. Back and forth. "Bad day?"

"Great day," Bailey replied. "Scary last hour."

When Elena released him, Dillon felt the absence like an unexpected sorrow. She slipped into Dillon's office chair and bundled her knees up under her chin. "What happened?"

"Later." Bailey kept her firm hold, but lifted her

head back far enough to see his smile. "What's so funny?"

"Crazy thought," he replied. "I feel like my arms were made for what just happened."

"Right answer." Bailey settled her head back on his chest. She asked her daughter, "Did you tell him?"

Elena started swinging the chair in tight little mini-rotations. "Not yet."

"So tell, honey. I thought that was why you came."

When Elena's only response was to continue her little chair-dance, Dillon asked, "Tell me what?"

Elena came out with something that sounded to Dillon like, "Iusedyourideaandfinishedthethingieand sentitoffandnowImtryingnottofreak."

He felt Bailey shift slightly, and knew it was time to release his hold. Hard as that was. Dillon leaned against the desk and said, "Bailey, a little help here."

"To translate from pre-teenese, Elena used your concept—"

"It wasn't my anything," Dillon protested.

"Don't interrupt the mayor," Elena said. "She'll puff up with all the words she hasn't gotten out and explode all over us."

"As I was saying, my darling daughter worked all night—"

"Ignoring yells from dear old Mom, who inter-rupted every hour on the hour."

"—and most of today. She finished her application and sent it off."

"And now I'm doing a major freak because they're taking forever to respond," Elena said.

"My darling genius, they haven't even read it yet."

"They're working to one clock. I'm living by another."

Dillon said, "This is fantastic news."

Bailey said, "Now is the moment when you thank the nice gentleman."

Dillon said, "She just did." He liked how Elena gave him one of those looks only a woman could manage, where the eyes were two bottomless wells. "That was the nicest thank-you I have ever had."

They remained trapped like that for what felt like hours. Happy in one another's company, no one ready to let the moment go. Until a large vehicle lumbered into the front drive, doors slammed, and voices laughed their way toward the station. Bailey said, "Here comes the fire chief."

"He's going to call me Lizzy," Elena said. "Why did you ever tell him my middle name?"

"It sort of slipped out," Bailey replied. "When I was yelling at you. Over something really important. Give me a minute and I'll remember what it was."

"Huh," Elena replied. "Not that important."

The office door slammed back and Charlie shouted, "Lizzy!"

Elena told Dillon, "I hate that name worse than spinach."

Bailey took two steps away from Dillon, and in that slight movement she switched from warm and caring to full-on mayor. "I have some news." She pointed out the side window to where the police chief was greeting volunteers. "Porter needs to hear this too."

Charlie protested, "I'm not sure this day can hold anything grim."

"Just the same, you both need to hear it."

"Can it wait until tomorrow?"

"Not a chance in the whole wide universe."

"Bailey—"

"Now means now."

When the station chief stepped out, Elena said, "Mom's been practicing that voice on me. For years."

"Only when you need it." When Porter joined them, Bailey said, "Close the door."

Charlie sighed. "I was having the first good day in years."

"I can't tell whether this news is good or bad. Only that it can't wait." Bailey took a breath. "The governor is coming to Miramar."

24

Olivia was helping Maud clean and prep the jail cells when Bailey rushed in. The mayor led Olivia out front, dropped her gubernatorial bombshell, and said, "Dillon says you're the perfect pro to help us develop before-and-after images of the damage. The question now is, can you fit yourself around a timeline that just got shrunk to almost nothing."

"I can work fast," Olivia replied. "And Gleason can help with the befores."

"In that case, you're it." Bailey walked to the nearest desk, grabbed pad and pen, and scribbled. "Here are what I'd class the six most crucial areas where we need federal funding. Consider these just a starting point. Add whatever you think of." Bailey handed her the page. "And hurry."

*   *   *

Despite the mayor's sense of urgency, Olivia took her time walking down Ocean Avenue. This particular late afternoon was already so full of so much. What she needed most was a chance to revisit the conversations she'd just had.

Her and Dillon. Dillon and the builder, Berto Acosta. Olivia and the mayor.

Go for it? She had actually said that to Bailey?

And meant it? Really?

Yes, as a matter of fact, she had.

The lance of regret she had felt was just that. A momentary spasm. Or so she tried to tell herself. And hoped desperately it was true.

Olivia spent the next couple of hours in Gleason's back room, going through his photo files. He had stored computerized renderings of many bygone favorites. She took her time, enjoying this glimpse back into the world she had known as a child. Once she had selected the early photos, she matched these to contemporary images of Miramar at its best. She then made a mental note of areas she would photograph the next morning, illustrating both the damage and the need.

But as she finished up, Olivia kept being struck by a niggling doubt. She had the distinct impression that she was missing a vital element. What that might be, she had no idea.

Gleason was busy in the front room dealing with multiple pre-Christmas clients. Olivia left a note on his desk and slipped through the shop and headed out. As she started up Ocean Avenue beneath a slate evening sky, she realized she was famished.

She was surrounded by a mist shifting in random waves. The Pacific was louder today, emitting a sullen growl that accompanied her up the gentle slope. A larger storm was out there somewhere, probably headed their way.

Most families previously trapped in Miramar had left. It was just the locals now. She walked the side alley and knocked on the diner's kitchen door. "Anybody home?"

"Huh. That's a good one." Claire appeared in the doorway. "As if we had time to be anywhere else."

"Come on in, darlin'." Arnaud offered his nearly constant smile. "Sorry, we're all out of rodents. The traps came up empty."

"Hush with your rodents," Claire said. To Olivia, "The boats went out. We've got line-caught mahi."

With flour-spackled arms, Arnaud pointed to orderly counters. "Tonight's special is grilled mahi tacos with cilantro, cabbage slaw, and my mother's special sauce."

"His mother is a worse cook than me," Claire said. "Nix on the sauce."

Olivia said, "I'd love some, thank you very much."

"We've also got tables out front, if you're interested in actually being comfortable," Arnaud said.

Olivia seated herself on a stool. "What I'd most like is a chance to chat."

"Goody. I've been looking for an excuse to take a break." Claire picked up a double armful of plates and headed out. "Let me deposit these and check my tables, and I'm yours."

Her friend returned just as Olivia finished a second portion. "Good?"

"Wonderful."

"Coffee?"

"Perfect."

Claire filled two mugs, set them on the counter, then pretended to inspect Olivia. "I don't see any gaping wounds." She settled onto the next stool. "If they were demolishing the cottage where I grew up, I'd be a basket case."

"Actually, I haven't given it much thought," Olivia replied. "And that's not what I wanted to talk about."

"Really?"

"Yes. And they're not tearing it down."

Arnaud offered, "That's not what we've heard."

"They're moving it. At least for now. And the cottage is not the issue. Well, of course, it is. But it's not at the head of today's shopping list."

"So what . . ." Claire realized her husband had sidled in so close he was almost touching. "Don't you have something that needs burning?"

"It can wait. Go on, Olivia darlin'. What's on your mind?"

Claire told her, "Say the word, I'll shoo him back to the far corner."

"Actually, it'd be nice if you both stayed," Olivia replied. She took a huge breath, announced, "Bailey is in love with Dillon."

They both froze. And might have remained that way for hours, if Claire's other waitress had not pushed through the kitchen door and called, "New table of five. All want the special."

"On it," Arnaud said. "Olivia, talk loud." He rushed over and began filling plates.

Claire demanded, "You think or you know?"

"I saw how she was watching Dillon. We spoke. She confessed."

Arnaud passed over the plates and bounced back. "Bailey Long. Our mayor."

Claire said, "Bailey told you she's in love with the man who broke your heart."

"Right. Him."

Arnaud said, "The guy you're going to be living with."

"Not like that I'm not."

Arnaud told his wife, "She doesn't sound broke up to me."

"I'm sorry," Claire said. "Obviously my brain is operating in the wrong gear. You're actually telling us you are okay with them being, you know, together?"

Olivia replied, "I told her to go for it."

The waitress reappeared. "Claire. Table eight wants dessert."

Arnaud said, "Maybe we should just close for the day."

"Tempting, but no." Claire rose from her stool. "Don't anybody say a single solitary word until I get back."

Arnaud retreated to the stoves, worked his way through a couple of orders, dinged his pickup bell, prepped more plates. Claire came and went twice. Olivia found it mildly amazing, how they could both continue with their jobs while apparently looking nowhere except at her.

Ten minutes later, husband and wife were back. Claire said, "Hon, what exactly are you wanting to discuss?"

"I'm trying to figure out why I feel the way I do."

"Okay," Claire said. "The light is beginning to shine."

Arnaud shook his head. "See, that's why I leave the room when you and your lady friends start talking about guys."

"I'll try and explain later," Claire told him. "Again."

Olivia said, "I love Dillon. He's a part of my life. I

hope he always will be. When I arrived back and saw him, I mean the very instant we met up, I felt like all the years just vanished."

Claire said, "All those years, meaning while you were married to old what's-his-name."

"Exactly. It felt like I hadn't allowed myself to miss Dillon until that moment. When we were back together again."

"That is just so sweet," Claire said.

Arnaud said, "Okay, now I'm really lost."

Claire ignored her husband. "So you come back for the first time in forever. You discover your home is a wreck. Porter offers you a bed inside his jail. And wait, who is in the next cell but the heart-breaker himself."

"Right."

"So you're concerned that all this might, just might, be warping your judgment."

"Yes and no."

Arnaud opened his mouth, but Claire raised one finger, halting words before they emerged. Which Olivia thought was remarkable, given how Arnaud stood directly behind his wife and Claire's gaze was laser-focused on her friend. Claire told her, "I'd say you were perfectly right to be worried. Now tell me what you think is going on here."

"I don't know." Olivia thought her voice sounded overly calm. As if internally she wailed, but didn't know how to release her confusion. "I need you to tell me what you think."

Arnaud wheeled about, waved his arms over his head, and went back to the stoves. The clattering pots almost masked his muttering.

Claire glanced at her husband, smiled, said, "That's a good little chef." Then she told Olivia, "Do you love Dillon?"

"I always will. But I don't *love* him."

Claire's smile was as gentle as a mother inspecting her infant. Sharing a special moment. Just the two of them. "You think or you know?"

"I'm growing more certain by the moment. And I desperately want this to be true. Especially, you know . . ."

"Since you just told our childhood bestie to go for the cheese."

Struggling to express these partially formed thoughts had an interesting effect. Olivia felt as though she listened to herself, but as an outsider. Watching the concepts take full form only as she spoke. "Coming up here, I really thought my life was over. I'd hit the brick wall, and the best I could hope for was to limp back home." She watched Arnaud walk back and fit himself in beside his wife. Spatula in one hand, empty taco shell in the other. Olivia continued, "Take my time, do what I could to survive and hopefully heal. Someday. Maybe."

Arnaud spoke with grave authority. "You're talking like a lady with no friends. Which isn't the situation here. At all. You hear what I'm saying?"

Claire slipped her arm around Arnaud's waist. Gave him a one-arm hug. Asked Olivia, "And now?"

"Ever since I arrived, I've watched new avenues open up. New opportunities." She took a hard breath. "I'm happy. It's a word I haven't used to describe myself in what feels like centuries."

"Now you're talking," Arnaud said.

Claire said, "Back to Dillon."

The reality she faced became clear. This was why she had come here, Olivia now knew. To speak these words aloud. And accept them as her version of truth. She desperately hoped. "I'm just a few months removed from my divorce. Not to mention attending my ex's funeral. Losing my business. And my home. You see?"

This time, it was Arnaud who nodded. "This is a perfect case of bad timing. You're not ready. Not for the old to become new." When Claire turned and looked at him, he said, "What?"

"Oh, nothing." She kissed him soundly. "My kitchen poet."

Olivia said, "Actually, it feels like *great* timing."

Arnaud stepped away. "Okay, now I'm back inside that total guy-confusion zone."

The other waitress chose that moment to enter the

kitchen and announce, "Looks like half the town council just arrived. And they're hungry. And they're asking about the lady here. And they've got the heart-breaker with them."

Claire scolded, "You weren't supposed to be listening to a private conversation."

The waitress was tall, strong, weary, and very amused. "Honey, that's the only way I keep myself entertained."

Arnaud turned back to his stove. "Rodents on toast coming up."

Claire rose, hugged her friend, said, "Go see if all those good intentions stand up to watching the two of them together."

25

When Olivia entered the diner's front room, the mayor was seated at the head of a table holding seven places. Bailey listened intently as Porter and Charlie and Berto talked, heads together, smiling. Like they were working together on something that made them all happy. Despite everything.

Dillon was seated at the table's other end, equally intent, and just as happy. Paying the trio no mind whatsoever. Not even glancing in Olivia's direction. His attention was totally focused on a girl of perhaps ten or eleven years of age, yet who held herself as someone much older. She could only be Bailey's daughter.

The woman-child had a tablet on the table between them, scrolling through a written document. Dillon had one hand on the back of the girl's chair, totally locked in on whatever he read. He nodded slowly while Bailey's daughter watched him, a smile coming and going.

Bailey's daughter was so totally smitten by Dillon.

And apparently Dillon felt the same about her.

There was no other way to describe what Olivia saw. This was a reality so potent it reshaped both their worlds.

She watched Dillon lean forward and spoke softly, patting the girl's shoulder in time to his words. Whatever he said caused Bailey's daughter to tear up. She smiled in response, looking at him with what Olivia could only describe as a womanly gaze.

That was the point at which Bailey pulled out the empty chair next to hers and said, "Aren't you joining us?" She waited until Olivia was seated, then said, "We're talking about first steps in regards to your cottage."

"We need to get everything in place before the armada invasion," the fire chief agreed. "Which means starting at first light."

As they resumed their discussion, Olivia knew she should be paying attention. But she remained captivated by Dillon and Bailey's daughter. Watching the two of them, the former love of her life and this young woman, there was no question in her mind. Dillon had changed for the better.

But what about her?

Olivia nodded to the gathering, as if they had posed the question. That was the true issue.

The answer was, she had no idea.

Her heart remained wounded by everything crammed and pounded into the past six months. One massive blow after another, severing her ties to LA, sending her back to Miramar. With nothing. Or so she had thought.

Yet here she sat, surrounded by people who wanted only good for her. Who stood ready to help in any and every way possible.

Her mind flashed back to a long-forgotten moment. One she had not thought of in years, yet was suddenly clearer than the people surrounding her.

Olivia had broken up with Dillon. Again. Bailey and her fiancé had been on the outs for weeks. That particular day, Bailey had approached her and asked if Dillon was a free agent. That was how she had expressed it. Like a pro ballplayer cast aside by his team. If so, Bailey wanted Dillon to take her to something. A dance, maybe. Party. Whatever. Olivia had seen the spark in Bailey's gaze, and known instantly this was not some chance encounter, a possible stand-in for her absent beau. This was real. And the knowledge had driven Olivia back into Dillon's arms.

Bailey leaned in close, and whispered, "Why are you smiling?"

Olivia turned to the mayor, her friend since childhood. And spoke as if it was just the two of them seated there, with all the time in the world. "I was thinking about that day you asked if Dillon and I were through."

Bailey tilted her head, a habit Olivia had seen hundreds of times. Checking out her world from a new angle. "You still remember that?"

"It just popped into my head. You wanted him to take you somewhere."

"Santa Cruz. My cousin's wedding."

"I should have let it happen."

The rest of the table might have sailed off into the far distance. Bailey softly replied, "Woulda shoulda."

Olivia nodded. The steps she could have taken, versus the ones she chose, stretched out before her. Like the choice was here in this very moment. "I knew even then it wasn't working with Dillon. But I wasn't ready to let him go. Which I probably should have." She paused, then asked, "Why am I only seeing this now?"

Bailey remained silent.

"What I wanted was for Dillon to be a different person. Does that make any sense?"

"Huh." Barely a whisper. Glancing at her daughter. Then resuming her tight focus on Olivia. "Does it ever."

Olivia leaned in closer, just inches removed from the woman's face. "I wanted to change him into the man who would leave with me. He wanted out as much as I did. But his direction . . ."

"Different compass heading."

Olivia shook her head. "His way didn't include me. Looking back, I think I already knew that."

Bailey did not blink. Or breathe.

Olivia went on, "But you wanted him. I saw it. And I was so jealous, I went straight to Dillon and apologized, said our breakup was all my fault. For the first time ever. Maybe the last."

Bailey said, "Did it ever occur to you that you saved me a ton of sorrow? Getting together with Dillon would have been the worst move ever. He wanted nothing more than to put Miramar in his rearview mirror. I was never going anywhere. Never, never, never. This is home. Then, now, tomorrow."

Olivia did not reply.

Bailey must have found what she sought in Olivia's silence. She took a firm hold of Olivia's hand and whispered, "Girl, thank you."

Charlie Hurst called from the table's opposite end, "What are you two scheming over down there?"

"Making sure my pal knows she has a home," Bailey replied. "Come what may."

26

They all left the diner together, a laughing, jostling, weary, excited group.

Then together they all froze. Bailey and Elena and Berto and Emelia and Charlie and Maud and Dillon and Olivia. They stood in a velvet dusk, not a breath of wind, the air shining with the sunset's ethereal light.

The *sunset*.

The clouds bunched tight over the northern horizon, a portent of another storm possibly coming their way. But just then they were silenced by a wonder that Olivia thought could only be described as glorious.

Claire must have seen how they stood, seven faces pointed straight up, mouths open in wonder. She stepped out, then returned inside and called to her husband. Thirty seconds later the two of them emerged, along with the waitress and most of the other patrons.

The evening star shone in a crystal clear sky, a single beacon of a hope so powerful Olivia actually shed tears.

Then they heard voices.

Footfalls took the place of falling rain, a soft patter that built as more and more people joined them, everyone headed toward the sound.

They climbed three blocks, took the turning, rushed past the town hall and fire station, and arrived.

The street in front of the old Catholic church was jammed. More people arrived with every passing moment. They were met with volunteers passing around song sheets. Others handed out candles whose bases were wrapped in little paper sleeves to protect the holders from dripping wax. The gathering was led by the town's vicars, standing on the church's porch, keeping time. Candles were lit, places found in the music, and together they all joined in.

It came upon a midnight clear, that glorious song of old.

27

Exhaustion proved a potent elixir. Olivia slept deeply and awoke to an empty cell. Voices sounded from the station door's other side, but where she lay all was quiet. She rose and dressed and padded into the main station, where a large woman with flashing eyes greeted her with a steaming mug. "I was just about to bring you this. You saved me a journey into nightmare territory."

Maud said, "Emilia has a thing about jails."

"As would anybody with a proper brain in their heads," Emilia replied.

Maud looked over. "Excuse me?"

"Present company excepted, of course." Her smile was a glorious thing, huge and illuminating. "You must forgive me, Maud. I'm merely excited about saving this lovely woman from her present fate."

"Actually, that's exactly what the jail has done for me," Olivia offered. "Saved me from being stranded in the storm."

"There, see?" Maud resumed her work. "You're welcome back any time, hon."

Emilia sniffed. "Well, that was then and this is now. My Berto has a home for you. Isn't that wonderful news, Maud?"

"Great." Maud punched her keyboard with renewed force. "Yay."

Olivia said, "You're Berto Acosta's wife?"

"Of course. Didn't I say that?"

"Actually, no."

Maud offered, "She forgets herself now and again, does Emilia."

Emilia went on, "Berto left with his crew hours ago, which is silly, since my husband won't do anything but stand around shouting orders while the crew does the real work. So here I am, playing stand-in, ready to show you your new home."

Olivia found herself struggling to keep up. "Berto is up working on my cottage?"

"She left that part out too," Maud said, then added, "Bailey's gone up too. She stopped by here an hour or so ago and collected Dillon."

Olivia decided now was a good time to retreat. "I need my gear. Bailey's given me a list of things she wants photographed."

"Speaking of my dear friend the mayor . . ." Emilia followed her into the jail. She stopped in the cell's entry, shuddered, then asked, "If you want my advice, you need to watch out. Bailey has what I'd call a wandering eye."

"It's not wandering." Olivia opened her camera case, selected the Canon body, fit on her most flexible zoom, and stood. "Bailey is head over heels in love."

Emilia's gaze widened. "You're okay with this?"

"I think it's wonderful," Olivia said, and was both delighted and relieved to discover she meant it.

"Well." Emilia started back down the central corridor. "This has all the makings of a good telenovela. Which I positively adore. You must tell me everything."

Emilia insisted they stop by the diner's rear door for breakfast burritos and more coffee. Olivia filled in portions of the recent Dillon saga between bites. The woman proved to be a wonderful listener, gasping softly in response to the more salacious bits, humming a sorrowful note at Olivia's reasons for returning. Claire stood in the doorway, arms crossed, smiling to Olivia's retelling. When they were done, Emilia ignored Claire's protests, stuffed bills in the woman's apron, and declared, "We're off."

Emilia possessed a flexible accent, one moment speaking with a flat Californian resonance, the next almost singing to some internal salsa. "We have so many nice people moving into Miramar. You will soon have many new friends. And Berto likes your young man very much." She touched a finger to her lips, denting her grin. "Next time I must correct these words before they emerge."

"It's okay. I have the same problem."

"See? You are living proof that the currents of life can be altered." She pointed ahead as they started down the lane between the guesthouse and the coffee shop. "Do you remember this area?"

"Dillon had a friend who lived back here." Small shops gave way to a rubble-strewn park. On the opposite end, teens played a noisy game of basketball. Every basket was marked by a rattling of the chain-link net. "He used to call it 'where bad people came looking for trouble.'"

"Those days are gone," Emilia declared. "Thanks to Porter and the town council and good people who want to see things change. Before the storm, this park was to be our next big challenge. Now such things must wait. But not for long. You mark my words."

Olivia found herself liking the woman immensely. "Where are we going?"

"You'll see. Back to Berto and the young man who is no longer yours." She offered an impish smile. "See? You are not the only one who can change course. Now we must discuss tomorrow. Berto hears they want Dillon to become the new auditor. Town and county both." She glanced over. "The question, the concern, is how long this Dillon plans to remain."

Which seemed the proper moment to share what

she knew of Dillon's recent past. The story took them along several more blocks of low-slung houses, some beautifully kept up, others as decrepit as the park. Emilia turned down one side street, another, winding their way farther from the town's heart.

Finally Emilia halted at the boundary of a rain-sodden construction site. The building project covered all of one block and much of the next. Raw earth and piles of construction materials glistened under the looming gray sky. "This is my darling man's dream project." Emilia pointed to a lone house rising in the second block's far corner. "That is to be his show home."

It would have been all too easy to discount the cottage entirely. The yard was raw earth, its neighbors were three skeleton frames, the drive unfinished. But as to the home itself, Olivia murmured, "Lovely."

"This neighborhood has been Berto's passion since forever. One I share. We both grew up here. Back then, it was a good place. People worked hard, kids played safely in the streets, friendships were strong, families stronger." She stared at the empty block, remembering. "Time has not been nice to our neighborhood. We want to change that."

The cottage was a modern rendition of the Craftsman style. The simple whitewashed exterior was brightened by pale-wood frames around the windows and matching pillars fronting the broad porch.

"It will be noisy," Emilia warned. "Sunrise to sundown."

"We can live with that," Olivia said. "Definitely."

"Berto will finish your neighbors next. He says three months should do it, once the rains end. Until the next home is live-in ready, he wants to use your place as his show home." Emilia glanced over. "You and your former young man will be okay with this?"

"I can't speak for Dillon. But my guess is, he'll be thrilled."

"The power company promises this neighborhood will have power fully restored by this evening. Berto hopes they can have water turned on tomorrow, two days at the most." Emilia smiled. "Of course, this is a builder who is making these promises. At Christmas time. After these storms."

"I understand." Olivia studied the home and recalled, "When I was little, Mom used to take me on these long wandering drives. She'd stop at homes like this and say something like, 'One day.'"

As Emilia started to respond, her phone chimed. She glanced at the screen, and abruptly started away. "So it's settled. Now we must dash."

"Wait, what about seeing inside?"

"No time, no time!" She was almost running. "Hurry!"

28

Olivia followed Emilia back along the same route they had taken, one step off a full run. Up ahead was a growing cacophony—people shouting through loudspeakers, sirens wailing, music blaring, crowds laughing and shouting back. A complete and utter transition from the rainy silence that had defined Miramar since her return.

The basketball courts were empty save for two balls lying forlorn and forgotten. Doors opened as they passed. People called inside and shouted at neighbors and joined the mad rush.

Ocean Avenue was alive with gawking, confused locals. Olivia thought she recognized many of the faces, faint glimmers back to an earlier time. But what made it all different, what was truly special about the moment, were the smiles.

It was a parade only in the sense that there was a

noisy procession of vehicles. The town's fire engines came first, crammed with any number of men and women. Now and then a child raced up, arms outstretched, shouting words no one could hear. By the time the third truck trundled past, lights flashing and sirens whining, dozens of kids were onboard. They screamed laughter and waved at the growing crowds while dogs barked and their mothers shouted instructions the kids happily ignored. All the shops were empty now, all the sidewalks and side streets jammed, all the people confused and amused both.

Dillon rode atop the last fire truck, a red velvet Christmas cap slanted over one eye. A huge grin split his face. If Santa arrived by way of a pirate ship, he might have an elf resembling Dillon. And suddenly Olivia was laughing and crying both. Dillon had never been easy with his smiles. Seeing him this happy, completely abandoning the burdens he carried, gave the day a truly unique flavor.

Next came four squat ER vehicles, followed by six stained and battered power-company trucks. Portable loudspeakers and megaphones were strung along their roofs. As they passed, the music shifted from a Christmas carol to a rock song urging listeners to freak the system. While not in the best of taste, Olivia thought the tune totally fit the moment.

Berto and Gleason and Maud and Ryan and Porter

and Bailey walked alongside the last vehicle, all wearing Santa hats, handing out flyers. As he passed, Berto paused long enough to kiss his wife soundly.

Gleason's grin twisted his face into unaccustomed angles. He handed Olivia and the blushing Emilia a couple of flyers and yelled, "Never had this much fun without a hangover!"

She shouted, "What is going on?"

But Gleason had already passed her, singing along as the music shifted mid-song back to something Christmassy.

29

Dillon felt like a nine-year-old on a sugar high. His actual childhood home had held few such moments of carefree laughter. Even at that age, he had known things were not the way they should be. Escape through work, was how his grandmother put it. Starting the motel job had been one of the happiest days of his young life. Already taking aim at the exit.

And look at him now.

It was crazy, totally off the wall, being this happy in this town. Wearing a peaked red-velvet cap topped with a white pom-pom, riding on top of a worn-out truck, singing snatches of carols blaring from the makeshift speakers. Tossing handfuls of candy. Laughing with all the crew as kids shrieked and raced and were lifted on board. Being part of offering Miramar a reason to smile. Yelling *Merry Christmas!* to one and all.

Their parade served as a Pied Piper for so many locals. By the time they passed the town hall and approached the fire station, pedestrians and barking
dogs filled the lane.

And then Dillon spotted her.

Bailey stood on the town hall's top step, so happy
she did a little two-step, swinging her daughter's arm.
Elena kept trying to pull away, playing the cross
teenager even while she laughed. When Bailey spotted
Dillon, she released her daughter and waved both
hands over her head.

What happened next was the most natural thing in
the world. Dillon clambered down, dropped to the
street, raced up the stairs, and gave the mayor of Miramar what felt like the finest kiss of his entire life.

It seemed to him that the entire town cheered.

He stepped back far enough to look at Bailey and
her daughter. Both of them smiling at him. And something more. There was a shared light to their gazes.
Dillon had the sense that they both held the same secret thought. One that left them smiling and secretly
weeping at the same time.

Bailey said, "I want you to come inside." But when
he started back up, she raised her free hand, palm
out. "Not now. Everybody is watching. Later, okay?
My office."

"Sure thing." He raced back through a grinning crowd. Many hands reached out, patting his shoulders and back as he passed. It almost felt like they were welcoming him home.

Crazy.

For Olivia, this proved to be a transcendent hour.

She stood on the sidewalk surrounded by what felt like half of Miramar's total population. This was a locals-only sort of hour, friends calling to friends, children racing from one family group to the next, adults chatting and laughing as her family's old cottage was settled onto temporary foundations.

In the light of day, the storms' damage to her former home was laid bare.

The town's emergency vehicles used their sirens to crawl down the lane and park. The vacant lot alongside the fire station was filled with Berto's construction crew. They worked in noisy cheer, positioning her former home onto temporary foundations. At the lot's far end, the power company set up a pair of emergency generators. Berto surveyed the work from the safety of the station's drive. When his wife joined him, the builder pulled an elf's cap from his back pocket, planted it on Emilia's head, ignored her protests, bent her back in a Latin's mocking ardor, and kissed her soundly. The laughing throngs considered it fine entertainment.

Olivia watched as Dillon bounded back through the crowd, jostled and applauded as he made his way toward her. He moved in close enough to be heard over the music still blasting down the lane and asked, "Are you okay with this?"

Olivia had no idea whether he meant her former home's new status, or the kiss he had just landed on Bailey. And decided it really didn't matter. "Better than okay."

"Really and truly?"

Suddenly she faced the old Dillon. The man she had once been madly in love with. The guy she was meant to spend her life with. Or so she'd thought. During the good times. And there were so many of those.

Dillon was happy and excited and full of the fire that seemed to ignite everyone within reach. Especially her.

He also carried a sorrow that rendered him timeless, at least in Olivia's eyes. Restless and full of passion. The draw was simply magnetic.

Just the same, she felt her mind and heart take a giant step back. There was no need for her body to move. Her life was already on a different course.

She said, "Without the slightest shred of doubt."

He must have found what he sought in her gaze. Dillon hugged her, a tight and fleeting embrace, then said, "I need to go help out."

She smiled him away. Feeling eyes on her. Knowing Bailey and her daughter were watching. Which was totally okay.

Friends.

30

Dillon spent the next hour serving as one of several messengers. He and Berto and Charlie and Emilia and Porter and Maud and Ryan circled through the crowd, inviting people to bring their unused Christmas lights and help decorate the cottage. The drumming generators added soft emphasis to their request. He met any number of people who claimed to have known him, though most of the faces were unfamiliar. Now and then he glanced at the town hall's front porch, where Bailey remained deep in serious conversations. Elena was seated in one of the porch chairs, long legs sprawled in pre-teen ease, working her phone. There was no need for Dillon to hurry back.

Besides which, he was having fun.

He had never felt as close to the people of Miramar as he did now. Most faces remained creased with the weary remnants of everything they and their hometown had endured. But now, two days before Christmas, there was a renewed illumination to many gazes. A grand reason to smile, to enjoy the hour and the season. At long last.

As he circulated and repeated the message, Dillon felt like he was being released from the cage of his past few months. He was still bruised, of course. Just like these locals. But he also shared their determination to wrest what happiness he could from this rare moment.

He looked up in time to see Bailey gesture to her daughter, lifting Elena from the chair. The two of them glanced his way, then vanished inside.

Dillon gave it a moment, then started over. As he climbed the front stairs, he was filled with a sense of momentous change.

The two women watched Dillon's approach through a window occupying the door's upper half. The mayor's office was set behind the empty front office. Something about their somber expressions had his heart racing. Dillon took their silent watchfulness as the only invitation he was probably going to get. He opened the door, stepped inside, and asked, "What's wrong?"

"Have a seat."

Elena occupied the mayor's office chair, her legs tucked up so her chin could rest on her knees. If anything, her expression was bleaker than Bailey's. Dillon replied, "I'm okay standing."

"If you wish." She crossed in front of him, locked the door, and pulled down the blind. "I have to ask you something."

"All right."

Bailey took up station in the middle of the office, arms crossed, and demanded, "When are you leaving Miramar?"

The way Bailey phrased it caused her daughter real pain. And Bailey knew it. But she did it anyway. Not if. When. Offering Dillon the open door.

He chose his words very carefully. "I left. I've come back. End of story."

"Is it, Dillon? Really?"

"I had to go. It was the only way I could ever return."

"To leave again," Bailey said. "Once you've recovered."

The words hung there in the space between them. "I'll never go back to what I once had. That door is closed. Permanently."

"That's not what I meant and you know it."

Dillon remained silent.

Bailey continued, "What happens when some lure is dangled in front of your face? Another perfect reason to escape. That's what I want to know."

Dillon thought his voice sounded exactly like hers. Soft, toneless, almost drone-like. The emotions were too potent to be expressed in any other way. "Things have changed."

"Have they."

"Yes."

"In what way?"

The questions he had carried since his return crystallized into a memory he had not thought of in years. "My grandad was quiet by nature. We could spend an entire day together, me chattering away, him not saying a word. The day before I left for business school, I worked the vineyard with him. That was my way of saying good-bye. As we walked back, he told me I needed to find a good woman who would point the way ahead. Which was a shock on many levels. My grandparents never mentioned Olivia. Of course they saw the results of our arguments. But they never spoke about us or her. Not once. And here was my grandad, the quietest man on earth. Talking about my needing a woman to help me find my compass heading. I didn't ask if he was talking about Olivia because I didn't need to."

Talking through the experience crystallized the recollection. Dillon recalled how tired he'd been, standing in the home's rear yard, sweat-stained and filthy, his pruning shears resting on one shoulder. At that moment, Dillon realized his grandfather's attention had been captured by his wife. Dillon's grandmother was washing vegetables she'd just taken from their garden in the outdoor sink. Dillon was so involved in the recollection it took him a moment to find his voice and continue. "He said there would probably come a time when I needed to change my life's course. And I would only do that when I had learned to trust the right woman. Whether I liked it or not, whether I agreed or not. I would do what she told me, out of love."

Bailey's only response was to cross the room and stand behind her desk. She settled her hand on Elena's shoulder. Her daughter responded by taking a firm hold on Bailey's hand.

What Dillon saw in those two faces filled him with a rock-solid certainty. "Over the past few months I felt like my world was torn apart. Now I know that's only small component of the truth. Because my life has always been fractured. I've spent my life running. Trying to escape the cage of my early years. It's only now, looking at the two of you, that I feel a very real hope of healing."

Elena used her free hand to cover her eyes. Heaved a broken breath. Swallowed hard. Bailey looked down at her daughter, then back to Dillon. "What happens when you do heal?"

Dillon nodded, not so much at the question but at what Bailey was not asking. "I can't tell you what the future holds. All I know is, I love you both. And I never want to even think about having a day where we're not together. It's all so new, my world is so uncertain . . ."

That was as far as Bailey let him go. She rushed around, gripped his face with both her hands, pulled him down, kissed him. Hard.

The endless, blissful moment was interrupted by another warm form slipping in beside them, and a young voice whispering, "Group hug."

31

Settling Olivia's former home onto its temporary foundations took hours. Not that she minded. Olivia drifted around the crowd's perimeter, taking photographs of people and structures both. For the second evening in a row, the sky cleared as the sun descended. The light allowed Olivia to photograph the town's structures with an odd mixture of clarity and compassion. The fire engines and emergency vehicles gleamed with a weary determination, or so it seemed. She pulled a chair from the fire station and settled at the point where the station's cement yard met the street. A few minutes passed, then her presence melted into the background. She used an adjustable telephoto lens, which allowed her to take in the entire vista, or narrow her focus, draw in tight, and shoot faces.

All the while, her mind ranged far and wide, a

happy tide of recollections and questions for which she had no answer. Nor in this one sweet moment did she need any.

An hour and a half later, Bailey found her still seated there. The light was a mere rosy hue above the western hills, and Olivia had drawn up her legs so her heels caught the chair's edge. She propped the camera on her knees to keep it stable. Bailey waited as she photographed a family depositing a collection of yard ornaments. A young boy proudly handed a huge plastic reindeer to a woman who smiled through her weariness. The pile she managed was almost as tall as the station.

Bailey said, "We're gathering for a meal at the diner. It might be a good idea if you join us."

"Great. I'm starving." She needed a minute to unlimber her legs. It felt better than good, having been so involved in taking photographs that she had ignored her growing discomfort. "Where's Elena?"

"Playing unpaid assistant." She waited as Olivia stowed her gear and shouldered the case. "Finding the others. Ordering them to drop everything and come now. Bossing adults is a job Elena was made for."

"Others?"

"Everyone who matters. Porter. Charlie. Gleason. Berto. Emilia. Maud." A minute hesitation, then, "Dillon."

They did not speak again until they entered the police station's parking area and Olivia deposited her camera case. As she closed the trunk, Bailey asked, "How has it been coming home?"

"Amazingly nice. I've found friends when I needed them most." She fell into step beside Bailey. "Before you showed up, I was remembering something I hadn't thought about in years."

"Terrible things, memories," Bailey said.

"Not this time." The light was dim now, the streetlights still out. The evening star shone astonishingly bright in the rain-washed sky. "Dillon and I had broken up. Again. Totally furious with each other. As usual. Then the anger faded, and I missed him so much." Olivia pretended not to hear the mayor's shaky breath and went on. "I couldn't stand being alone, so I walked up the hill. His father was there by himself, toking on his bong. So I climbed higher and found his grandmother standing where the boundary wall met the street. Dillon was working in the vineyard with his grandad. She must have seen me coming, and walked out to meet me."

"Where you two could talk and Dillon wouldn't hear."

"Exactly." They stopped where the diner's open rear door illuminated the lane. "I braced myself for the lady to tell me I should walk away. Leave her grandson in peace." It was Olivia's turn to take a hard breath. "I almost wish she had."

Claire chose that moment to emerge from the kitchen and say, "Bailey, they're all here."

"Tell them we'll need a minute." When Claire retreated, Bailey said, "Go on."

"She said Dillon's nature was potent and dangerous both. A sad and restless spirit was hidden beneath his wild energy and electric eyes. A potent mix, was the way she put it." Revisiting that moment was so intense, Olivia found it necessary to wipe her eyes. "She said it would either destroy him or carry him to greatness."

"Everything that happened didn't destroy Dillon," Bailey said.

"Far from it," Olivia agreed.

"It brought him home." Bailey studied her. "He's told us he doesn't want to leave. I believe him."

"That's not the issue here. At least, that's not why I mentioned it." Olivia pointed to the diner. "Right now he's sitting in there, coming to terms with who he is. Needing you to help him heal."

"Not you. Is that what you're saying?"

"Yes, but that's not the point either. Sooner or later he's going to be made whole. I think this new Dillon is bound to grow into what his grandmother saw all those years ago."

Bailey nodded slowly. "Greatness."

"How do you feel about that? Right now you're probably worried about him leaving Miramar again."

"I am. Yes." Bailey breathed. "A lot."

"What if he loves you enough to find peace in staying?" Olivia gave that a moment, then continued. "You're where you are because you want to lead. Can you be comfortable standing alongside a man who is also a force of nature?" Olivia liked how the woman remained silent. Thoughtful. Taking her words in deep. She could see it in Bailey's gaze. Finally she said, "Maybe we should join the others."

While they ate, the clouds gathered and rain fell. Not hard, more a persistent drizzle cast against the diner's windows by a fitful breeze. Everyone save Olivia watched the shift in weather. She used that as a chance to study them. The new-old friends who had done so much to shelter her through storms. They looked weary, strong, determined. All save Elena, who sat next to Dillon and positively glowed. Every now and then she leaned in close and whispered words meant only for him. He always responded with a different kind of smile, one so tender it lanced Olivia's heart.

Gleason noticed, of course. The older man was seated next to Olivia, and watched her watching them. "I go to sleep one night, and the next morning it seems like the world has shifted on its axis."

"Welcome to my life," Olivia said.

"So, you and Dillon . . ."

"Everybody's asking me that."

"Hardly a surprise. And?"

"We are friends for life."

"Friends," he repeated, his voice a soft, bearlike rumble. "Friends."

"Exactly." She decided now was a good time to change the subject. "Is there a particular reason why you're here?"

"I've been on the town council for a while. They recently appointed me deputy mayor." He offered a rare smile. "Everybody with more sense had already run for the hills."

Bailey chose that moment to tap her fork on the side of her plate. "If it's okay, I'd like to get started." When she had everyone's attention, she went on. "I've had two conversations with the governor's chief of staff regarding their visit tomorrow. There's good news and bad news. You need to help me decide which is which."

The diner was less than half full. Patrons at other tables watched and listened. Claire stood by the side wall, close to where Arnaud leaned on the counter and observed through the central window. Olivia suspected Bailey had chosen the setting for the purpose of getting the word out. The mayor went on. "The last couple of disasters, the feds were heavily criticized for taking too long to write the checks. FEMA has been under severe pressure to accelerate their process. They have decided the state's auditor will serve on point. Soon as he okays a budget request, FEMA will write the check. The feds will send in auditors to check our progress and spending. But Ransom Bates holds the key to getting what we need."

"Bad news," Gleason said.

"Terrible," Porter agreed.

"The man is not our friend," Emilia said.

"Point of order," Charlie said. "It's always a pleasure to see Lizzy—"

"Yuck."

"But why is your daughter here?"

"Elena is playing a very important role," Bailey replied.

"Is she, now."

"Absolutely. This is an official-unofficial meeting of the town council. Elena's job is to keep notes and write it all up."

"Funny," Charlie said. "I don't see a pad or pen."

Elena tapped the side of her head. "Click. Recording."

Dillon laughed out loud.

"Boyd Harrow, the governor's top guy, is doing what he can to protect us," Bailey went on. "The governor's PR team wanted a photo op that shows him working on Christmas Eve, personally helping one of the afflicted towns in their hour of need. And so forth."

"Smart," Emilia said. "Bringing in the top dog, letting the auditor know his bosses are watching."

Porter corrected, "Long as we give the governor and his PR folks what they want."

"That's our job in a nutshell," Bailey agreed. "He and his team will show up here tomorrow afternoon. Our job is to give them a quick sweep of the worst-hit areas, the points that are in dire need of the feds' help . . ." She stopped because Dillon stared at his plate, shaking his head. "What?"

He looked up. "Nothing."

"Go ahead and say it."

"I'm the guest here. I really shouldn't—"

Maud snapped, "You've somehow managed to crawl your way back into my good graces. Don't go wrecking your chances to stay there."

When he hesitated, Bailey added, "We're listening."

"Okay, so here's the thing. The governor's team is expecting us to show how Miramar is hurting."

"Which it is," Maud said.

"But they already know that. It's why they're coming. What if we tried to show them also how Miramar is *healing*?" He looked around the table, went on. "Olivia's been working on before-and-after photos. What if we use that as a starting point? Talk about our resilience, our determination to make things right?"

The mayor's daughter laughed, the sound bell-like.

Bailey nodded, though she shared none of her daughter's mirth. "This has promise."

Arnaud surprised them all by speaking through the kitchen window, "You're saying we should show them Miramar's heart."

"Why we love this place so much," Claire agreed. "Despite everything."

"I'm liking this," Porter said. He leaned back and inspected the ceiling. "I'm liking it a lot."

Bailey pushed her chair a fraction away from the table and studied the others.

"Maybe we should start by showing them the ocean walk," Dillon went on.

"Nothing's going to make a better photo-op," Porter agreed, addressing the ceiling.

"Bring him back to the fire station," Gleason said. "Walk him through our line of before-and-after photos."

Emilia demanded, "Can you get that ready in time?"

"Oh absolutely," Gleason replied. "We're already halfway there. Right, Olivia?"

"We don't need to show him everything," Berto said. "This isn't an inspection for the auditors."

And then suddenly everyone was talking. A great heave of excited planning. Olivia went heads down with Gleason, making notes of places she needed to start shooting at dawn. Then she looked up to find Bailey still watching Dillon.

32

Olivia and Gleason remained in the diner long after everyone else departed, working out a pictorial display of Miramar's heart. That was how Gleason framed their plans. The old grouch showing a different side as they worked. Passionate about his art, his town, the need to get this right.

As they started back toward the police station, Olivia fretted, "I'm still not certain the lineup will show—"

"You can just stop right there." Gleason watched her open the car trunk. "I never met an artist who knew how to hang their own work."

"You've never called me that before." She pulled out what she needed for the night, and added the last remaining set of clean clothes. "An artist."

"Well, you are, and you need to leave the framing and hanging to your betters."

"Now you sound like the grouch of my childhood."

"Lady, you do my heart good." Gleason frowned at the entrance. "You been okay staying here?"

"Better than that. It was my shelter in the storms. A lot of them." She kissed his cheek. "Good night, Mister Grouch, sir."

She left him there, touching the spot on his cheek, and went inside.

Olivia found herself continuing the dialogue as she prepared for bed. How she had arrived in Miramar so stripped bare the jail cell had suited her state. And yet, the longer she stayed here, the more she had discovered hidden gifts. As if the season had managed to find her even here, and bestowed upon her exactly what she needed.

Shelter, inside and out.

Friends, new and old.

A passion and a profession from her past, reworked to fit the woman she was now.

A new home.

A man she would always love. But never again in the way she had expected.

As she settled into her pallet, a thought came to her. One she sensed had been growing since that first walk she and Dillon had taken together. Yes, he had broken her heart. And part of coming home had meant facing the role she had played in making that happen.

All so she could close her eyes and snuggle into the covers, hearing him snore in the next cell.

Friends for life.

Olivia slept and did not dream.

33

Olivia was already up and moving when her phone alarm went off at half-past five. When she left her cell, perhaps for the last time, she saw Dillon had already departed. She dressed and entered the main station, greeted the sleepy deputy, and entered a silent dawn. She collected her camera case from the car and set off.

The sky remained shrouded, but the taste of coming rain was gone. The ocean was a distant rumble, a sound from her childhood. Olivia and her mother had often walked the Pacific pathway in the predawn hour, watching sunlight gradually take hold. Her mother liked to stop and listen to the ocean, calling it a hymn to better days.

Traces of cold Pacific mist began drifting inland as Olivia stood by the diner's rear door, enjoying a breakfast burrito. She wished Claire and Arnaud a lovely Christmas Eve day, and truly believed it might be so.

Thankfully, the morning mist did not strengthen to where it became impenetrable. Instead, thin veils touched the earth and moved on, leaving liquid jewels in their passage. She arrived at the parking area that marked the end of Ocean Avenue just as the sun rose above the eastern hills. Instantly the early morning mist became a golden veil, draping an ethereal glow over the battered shoreline.

Focus on the healing, Dillon had said. The idea resonated deeply. She thought it formed a wonderful challenge for everyone involved. Her challenge this morning was to photograph a town severely damaged by winter storms, yet determined to face its own new dawn. Just like her.

The question was, how? That was the quandary she and Gleason had discussed at length. Now, as she opened her shoulder-case and drew out the Canon and her adjustable zoom lens, she saw the answer.

Storm surf had chewed away the lot's leading edge, forming uneven steps in the rubble. Olivia made her way down to the sand, then used the drifting mist to camouflage her movements. When she was in position and the wrecked oceanfront path was turned mystical by the glowing veil, she dropped to one knee and began shooting.

She would not focus on the places. Nor the damage. The people were what made Miramar special. She would share images of people not just rebuilding the town, but restoring hope. After all, that was her gift. Her passion. Seeing the best in people, sharing it with the world.

She photographed three couples, all friends, who laughed as they pulled weathered planks from kelp that had been washed ashore. They stacked the timber by what was left of the ocean walk's central bridge.

When she had what she needed, she rose and backtracked and walked the beachfront road. She moved softly, trying to drift with the mist, intent upon going unseen. Three hundred yards later, she found her next shot.

An Asian lady of advancing years replanted orchids in the limbs of two live oaks. To her right stood a weathered tea house, the shattered windows sealed with plywood and cardboard and tape. An elderly man cleared rubble from the winding stone pathway.

Olivia captured the moment, then turned back and hurried inland.

Up Ocean Avenue, she photographed two men on ladders, repairing a roof gutter and stringing Christmas tinsel. A woman stood below them, pointing and directing and dodging ornaments they tossed in her direction.

Then the police station, where Maud and Porter

sat on a bench turned throne-like by the sunrise, sharing coffee and a weary smile.

Back behind the guesthouse and down a narrow lane, where she spotted her next shot. Olivia gained permission to crouch in one corner of a damaged home and shoot families welcoming neighbors into a warm and overcrowded kitchen.

Her final stop was the fire station. She had already decided to skip the people working around her former home. That would come later. Instead, she photographed the morning volunteers filling two pickups with food and water and presents. And hugs.

As she rushed back down Ocean Avenue, Olivia found herself recalling Bailey's thoughtful response to Dillon taking center stage. Worrying if Bailey would find peace in such a relationship . . .

Olivia halted in the middle of the empty street, lifted her face to the pale blue sky, and laughed out loud.

Here she was. Fretting over the man who had once occupied her heart's domain. Anxious about Dillon making a go of it. With another woman. Who, by the way, was perfect for him in so many ways. But still.

She arrived at Gleason's shop, opened the door, and declared, "I've had a very good morning."

34

Half past eleven, Dillon had been hard at it for almost six hours. He was tired, sweaty, and as happy as he'd been in a very long while. Elena had arrived two hours earlier and fit herself into Dillon's work like she'd been doing so all her life. His plan was simple enough, but the intricacies were daunting and they had very little time.

Bailey arrived soon after. She stood in the paved forecourt, sourly eyeing a massive pile of ornaments. The fire team and a horde of volunteers scurried around her, shouting and rushing. She entered the chief's office and declared, "We'll never be ready on time!"

"Charlie says they will," Dillon replied.

"One of the generators refused to start," Elena said. "They've brought in another."

"They couldn't position the lawn ornaments until the forklifts were gone," Dillon added. "Charlie thinks the pause might actually have helped. They had enough time to decide where everything's supposed to go."

"Remind me," Bailey demanded. "What are you two working on?"

Dilly replied, "We're almost done with the FEMA documents. We're doing a pictorial display of the major requests, thanks to Olivia. Gleason's going to bind it into booklets with photos to match. Give them something they can study on the way home." To Elena, "Where is Appendix One?"

"I have it."

"And the photos?"

Elena waved a sheaf over her head. "Chill, okay?"

Bailey asked, "Appendix One?"

Dillon replied, "Don't ask." To Elena, "Everything is in order?"

"Yes, yes, yes."

"Maybe I should check it one more time."

"No, no, no." She wiggled fingers in his direction. "Last folder. Gimmee."

"Please," her mother added.

"We left *please* about fifty miles back." Elena plucked the folder from Dillon's grasp, slipped in her pages, uncapped the felt-tip pen, and scribbled.

"That's folder seven," Dillon said.

"Yes, Dillon, I can still count. And yes, they are all numbered. And finally, yes, I have them in order."

Bailey asked, "Have you two eaten something?"

Elena said, "Claire stopped by with rodent stew."

"Breakfast burritos," Dillon corrected.

"Whatever." Elena hefted the stack of folders and ran for the door. "You children play nice."

Bailey watched her daughter scurry around workers sorting through the unkempt pile of ornaments, laugh at something Charlie shouted in her direction, and race down the street. "I can't remember the last time I've seen her so happy."

Dillon stared at the empty space where Elena had been working. "I've spent years thinking I was content to go it alone. I pretty much assumed any real need for a family had been cauterized by my childhood. You and Elena have sure proved me wrong."

"I'm sure someone has said something that nice to me before. Just now, though, I can't recall when it was." But her expression did not match her words. "Dillon . . ."

"What?"

"Nothing. It can wait."

"Tell me." He swept an arm around the empty office. "It's just us adults here."

She hesitated a moment longer, then pulled over a chair and seated herself just out of reach. Dillon started to inch closer, but something in her manner told him the move would not be welcome.

"Olivia was right. You're forcing me to rewrite my rule book," Bailey said. "I'm not sure I like that."

Dillon sorted through several responses, the process accelerated by how his heart rate had suddenly approached redline.

The first was, *You've discussed us and our relationship with the former love of my life?*

Next came, *There's a rule book?*

Finally, *Are you certain today of all days is when we need to be talking this through?*

For once in his rocky career as a guy ladies left behind, Dillon did the right thing and remained mute.

Bailey said, "The problem is, I can't tell whether I'm not liking your taking center stage, or that you're making me accept how so much of what's behind me is my fault."

Dillon decided his only course of action was to not blink, much less breathe.

"I watched you lay out a terrific idea to the team. *My* team. And they loved it. Which they should. Your plan could genuinely help my town heal." Bailey caught herself. "See, that's how hard you're making it for me. *Our* town."

Dillon remained silent. Frozen in place.

"But what I caught sight of just then, for one split second, was why I chose Griff. Why I made that relationship work despite the whole world telling me it was wrong from the start. The simple reason was, Griff was happy with me taking the spotlight. I led, Griff wandered. He never followed. He didn't care enough to be supportive. He just did what Griff always did. He went looking for the next . . ."

Bailey stopped and did a full-body clench. Fists to hairline. Everything went intensely tight. And in the process, the old pain aged her ten years.

She took a very hard breath, and willed herself to release. A smidgen. Not much. Enough to go on. "I have no idea how to be in a relationship with a man who is a genuine partner. I don't even know what those words mean. All I know is, I'm coming to love you. And I can't let my fears or my past or my natural desire to lead get in the way—"

She was silenced by a knock on the door. Porter opened and said, "Sorry to interrupt whatever this is. But we need to discuss—"

"Coming." Bailey started to follow the chief from the office, then turned back long enough to say, "I'm glad we had this talk."

Once the door closed, Dillon allowed himself to breathe.

35

Olivia served customers in the front room of Gleason's camera shop while her partner in crime ran off the necessary photographs. Every now and then Gleason emerged with another four or five prints, which she carefully attached with adhesive to a set of lightweight foam backings. Gradually the town's story and its determination to heal became stacked upon the counter.

There was a slow but steady stream of customers, mostly families doing late Christmas shopping. Olivia relished her role as adviser, which was what almost all of them were after. If these people had known precisely what they wanted, they'd have ordered online. Gleason's shop had changed with the times, and served a dual role now, selling phones and monthly plans as well as high-end photographic equipment. Two national companies ran competing shops of their own. It used to be four, according to Gleason, but the others recognized his sway within the community and licensed him instead.

Olivia loved her unexpected role. Especially when the customers included young people harboring an early passion. They were here because they wanted to move beyond selfies. They intended to shape art of their own. In an idle moment, Olivia found herself wondering if the old man might be interested in her taking on a more formal role. Here. Inside Gleason's solitary domain. The place which had played such a vital role in her own escape. All those many seasons ago.

Elena entered as Olivia concluded another sale. Bailey's daughter held a double-armful of manila folders and stood by the front window as the customers departed. When it was just the two of them, she remained frozen in place.

"Elena?"

Her only response was to tremble, tight little motions that rattled the pages in her arms.

Olivia rushed around the counter. "Honey, what's the matter?"

She showed Olivia frantic, wide-eyed gaze. "I just discovered what a panic attack feels like."

Olivia returned behind the counter, then rolled Gleason's chair over. "Here. Sit. Give me those files."

"These can't wait."

"Yes they can. Two minutes one way or the other

won't matter. Relax your grip, Elena." She took hold of the folders and started toward the counter, only to discover Gleason standing in the rear doorway. Olivia shoved the files into his arms and said, "We need a minute."

Olivia went back and squatted beside the young woman's chair. That was exactly how Elena seemed to her. A woman whose body had not yet caught up with the rest of her. Olivia asked, "Will you tell me what's wrong?"

"I'm so happy," she whispered. "And I'm so scared."

It seemed the most natural thing in the world to gather Elena in a heartfelt embrace. Then, "Don't wipe your nose on your sleeve, dear." She rose and pulled tissues from the box Gleason used for cleaning lenses. "Here."

"You sound like Mom." She sniffed, pulled a thumb drive from her pocket, said, "Gleason needs this too."

Olivia rose once more and entered the rear room. Gleason stood by the printer, watching, silent. Olivia told him, "Don't ask."

"Wasn't planning to." He accepted the drive, and handed her another half-dozen large prints. "This is the last of them. I never thought I'd say this to an artist. But you'll need to go hang them yourself." He started toward his desk. "Tell Dillon I'll have the booklets done on time. How, I have no idea. But I will."

Olivia started back, then stopped and said, "I've always wanted to ask. Is Gleason your first or last name?"

"It's the only name that matters."

"Oookay."

He scowled fiercely, an expression he had often used during Olivia's growing-up years. So potent it had silenced any number of teenage tirades. "My first name is Ramone."

"Get out of town."

"Named after a grandfather I never met."

"Gleason works just fine, thank you very much."

"Our secret, okay?"

"Absolutely. No problem at all. My lips are permanently sealed."

Helping Olivia apply the adhesive and position the final prints on their white backing steadied the young woman. The fiddling work required precision. Each photograph needed to be placed in the exact same position, so together they formed a unified flow. Elena measured, Olivia applied the adhesive-stick and placed each print, then Elena used the rubber-sided ruler to flatten each photograph. They could hear Gleason working in the back room. Neither woman spoke again until they gathered up the thirty-three prints, bid the old man farewell, and set off.

Once they were on the street, Olivia asked, "Is this about Dillon?"

Elena held the lightweight but oversize prints down low enough to see over the top edge. But this also meant they bumped her thighs with each step. "I feel stupid worrying about this with everything else we've got going on."

Olivia directed her smile at a pristine blue sky. "You want stupid, I walked down here worrying about your mom making a success of loving the man I once wanted to spend the rest of my life with."

They passed beneath a power-company crew repairing ornaments strung from the streetlights. Two families walking along the opposite sidewalk accused the crew of stealing Christmas. Elena said, "I will never understand adults."

Olivia felt a new level of awareness growing inside. One so potent she stopped in the middle of the sidewalk and studied the younger woman.

Elena demanded, "What?"

"I'm trying to decide if I can speak with you, woman to woman."

Elena liked that enough to nearly smile. "One way to find out."

"My relationship with Dillon is going through a

major change. Your mom might already have told you that."

"Not told, not really," Elena replied. "More like, she hopes that's happening. Really a lot."

"Well, it's true. And that's not the point. What's happening with Dillon is part of something bigger taking place in my life. I needed this chance to let go. Remove myself from yesterday." Olivia felt such a balloon filling her chest, so huge and so fast she had to force out, "It's the only way I can make room for whatever this new season might bring."

Elena offered a fractional nod. "Mom's been wrestling with that same problem. Letting go."

"Do you know anything about Dillon's early years?"

"Mom says they were rough."

Olivia started back up the sidewalk. The prints and their foam backing made a bulky but almost weightless armload. "A stoner dad, a mom who left when he was your age. Just walked out the door and never contacted her own son. Nothing."

"What I just said about understanding adults." Elena shook her head. "How can anybody do that?"

"Excellent question. Anyway, Dillon was saved by two things. His grandparents were the greatest. And Dillon loved to work. Still does. He took aim at building his own life and he worked to make it happen."

Elena added, "And he had you."

"Okay. Yes. Our good times were special and they helped. But we had a lot of bad times, and finally we broke up. And that's not the point here." Olivia was so intent upon the young woman she only now realized how the two of them had been joined by a number of others. Families, couples, young people, old, all walking in the same direction. She said, "Dillon never wanted kids. Whenever I brought up the subject, you know . . ."

"Back when things like that mattered," Elena said.

Olivia had to smile. Being so in synch with this woman-child was amazing. "Right. Dillon's reaction was a total negative. We fought about it so often. His response never changed. His desire for offspring had been cauterized by everything he'd been through."

"Lucky me," Elena said. Her attention was total now.

"Seeing the way he looks at you . . ."

"What?"

Olivia swallowed hard. Not from sorrow. Okay, well, yes, maybe, just a little. But mostly out of joy for her two friends. "You're the daughter he thought he'd never have. That's what I think. Elena, careful, don't drop the photos!"

"Sorry." She took a firm grip, lifted her face to the sky, blinked furiously. "Now I'm doing just like I always tell Mom not to."

Olivia continued. "It's too early for anyone to know how things will work out between him and

Bailey. But about one thing I am utterly, completely certain. You and Dillon are friends for life. He will be there for you. Always."

They turned the corner and entered a mob. Or so it seemed to Olivia. The street was filled from side to side with happy, jostling people. She started to thread her way forward, then Elena shouted, "Wait!"

When Olivia turned back, Elena was looking at her, eyes brilliant as washed gemstones. "Elena, honey . . ."

"I heard Mom talking with Dillon. I know you've been through a bad time. I just want to say, I'm pretty sure your storms had a reason."

Olivia had no idea what to say.

"Or purpose. Whatever. You and Dillon, you came when I most needed, and now you're here, and . . ." She lifted her head and shouted at the sky, *"This is the best Christmas ever!"*

Everyone within range turned and cheered.

Elena stepped around Olivia, who was still busy digesting what just happened. She yelled, "Coming through! Ladies on a mission!"

36

Dillon spotted them and pushed his way through the crowd. His smile and sheer unadulterated joy matched Elena's. He told the young woman, "I thought I heard your dulcet tones."

"That's not the words Mom uses when I yell."

"Hi, Olivia. You're late."

Elena said, "We got held up. Girl thingies."

"Let's get these inside." He nudged his way through the crowd, slipped around a makeshift barrier, and entered the fire station through the open bay doors. "They're here."

Bailey came rushing over. "Where have you been?"

"Making pretty pictures," Elena replied.

Olivia demanded, "Who are all these people?"

"Getting in the way!" Bailey wailed her response. "We'll never be ready in time!"

"Sure we will." Nothing seemed capable of disturbing Dillon's good mood.

"The governor will be here in . . ." She pulled out her phone.

But before she could continue, the entire fire station shouted in chorus, *"Three hours!"*

"Less," Bailey said. She shouted back. "Don't make fun of the mayor in meltdown!"

Which was when Elena handed Dillon her pile of photographs, slung her arms around her mother's neck, and declared, "I love you more than chocolate."

Bailey's mouth formed a perfect O.

Elena bounced back a step. "Everything's going to be great. Right, Dillon?"

"Absolutely."

Elena took the photographs back from Dillon and headed for the rear wall. She called to Olivia, "Come on, we've got a hanging to do!"

Bailey watched her daughter skip away, then turned to Olivia with, "Who is that mystery child, and what have you done with my daughter?"

"I'll explain later," Olivia said. She followed Elena, happy as she'd been in a very long while.

Together with Elena she laid out a basic concept, leaning the photographs against the rear wall, trying for what she thought of as emotive flow. They repositioned them several times, lining them as they talked through the process. Elena twice drew her mother over, supposedly to offer guidance. But Olivia suspected it was mostly so the two of them could argue.

After Bailey's second visit, they began measuring the placement and marking the walls. Elena insisted on measuring, and probably did a better job. She hummed fragments of a song Olivia did not recognize, then broke off to announce, "Mom says I'm not grateful enough. So thanks, by the way."

"You're most welcome."

Elena hummed a few more bars, then added, "What you said made me feel almost as good as talking to Dillon."

Olivia stepped back a few paces, and surveyed their planned structure. She decided they were ready to hang. "What did he say?"

"Pretty much the same thing. Only with math. Actually, I was the one with the math. Dillon just had the right answer. Sort of."

"Is it okay if I don't understand what you just said?"

"Oh, sure. I get that all the time." Elena stepped back and stood beside Olivia. "Are we after perfection or getting the job done?"

As if in response, Bailey chose that moment to yell, "Okay, people, listen up! The governor will be here in *two hours*."

37

Dillon followed Bailey back outside. The late afternoon sun was strong enough to begin drying out their world. The air was impossibly clean, the sky a fine China blue.

Bailey saw none of this. "What am I supposed to do with this mob?"

Dillon replied, "They're anything but."

"Maybe you're not seeing what I'm seeing."

"Bailey, these people are looking for a reason to party." He liked how she looked at him, trusting him enough to show her very real fear. "They've been cooped up since forever. Their town has been storm-hammered for weeks. They're gathering here because they want to be a part of whatever's coming."

She gave that a moment's silence, then, "Think you can handle them?"

"I guess. Is that what you want?"

"What I want . . ." A smile fought to break through her nerves. "I wish I could kiss you."

Which was exactly what he did. There in as public a setting as Miramar could offer. With what seemed like the whole town watching. And cheering.

Dillon was in his element. He stood behind the sawhorses framing the fire station's front area and studied the happy, yammering crowd. It was growing larger by the minute, as were the numbers of boxes and bundles of Christmas ornaments. The donations said it all. These people wanted to be part of whatever was happening. They wanted a reason to celebrate.

There had been times in his previous life when he had been the loner in a crowd. Traders and bosses were all caught up in a news alert that threatened to reshape their world. Everyone was looking for the direction to stampede. Dillon had loved those moments, being able to separate himself from the tension and fear and explosive energy. And do what he was doing now.

Porter stepped up beside him and observed, "You're the only guy here who's not in total panic mode."

"I'm just hiding it better."

"Maybe you should be a cop."

"Not on your life. No offense."

"None taken. Bailey said you might be needing a hand."

"Bailey's right."

As Dillon sketched out his half-formed idea, Gleason shouldered his way through the crowd carrying an overfull box. The shop owner announced, "Got your booklets."

"They're Bailey's," Dillon replied. "But thanks. A lot."

"You don't want to check them out?"

"No time," Dillon said.

"Yeah, you and the chief look super busy," Gleason scoffed.

"Thinking," Dillon said. "Planning. Doing what the mayor told me."

"Bailey's back inside," Porter said, pointing behind him. "Look for the lady on the verge of a total freak."

Dillon asked, "Once you've made your delivery, want to help us with crowd control?"

Gleason offered a very rare smile. "That's why I got into politics. So I could tell the town what to do."

Porter shook his head. "I try to avoid that at all cost."

"Just as well," Gleason replied. "Since nobody wants to listen to you anyway."

Over the next hour, Dillon fielded a dozen urgent issues. More. The crowd seemed more or less agreeable with the idea of a stranger giving them orders. Enterprising locals brought in mobile food vans. The power company shifted ornaments and lights from the powerless outer streets to the blocks of Ocean Avenue leading to their lane. Local musicians, including several semiprofessionals who backed up Connor Larkin, set up on the town hall's broad front porch— but only after they solemnly promised Dillon that every other number would be about Christmas. Gradually one side of the street began to take on the recognizable form of a street party.

The area around the fire station, however, was a very different story.

A bit later, he stopped for a coffee and fresh-cooked doughnut. Dillon stepped back far enough for the van to block him from most of the throng, granting him a much-needed breather. In the days and weeks to come, Dillon suspected he'd look back on this moment as his very own Christmas epiphany.

Standing there on the muddy rain-soaked earth, surrounded by the town and locals he'd fought so hard to leave behind . . .

He was as happy as he'd been in a very long while.

And something more.

Dillon felt genuinely fulfilled.

It wasn't coming home that did it. Or facing defeat. Or rising from the destructive flames. Or even standing on the verge of a new love.

It was all of those things. And more besides.

If Dillon had ever designed a motto for those years since leaving Miramar, it would have been, *Success first, life after*.

Or something to that effect.

And now, in the cacophony of a half-formed street party, he faced a future he could never have dreamed up. Not in a million years of yearning. Where there was nothing for him except the wonder of living this noisy, fractured, joyful day.

Which was when Bailey's daughter stepped in front of him and demanded, "Why are you hiding back here?"

"I'm not," Dillon replied. "I'm . . ."

Elena stood with hands on hips. "You're what?"

Dillon grinned. "Okay. Hiding works as well as anything I can come up with."

"Mom sent me over to make sure you weren't in a total panic. And if you are, she said to tell you that's her job."

Dillon stepped away from the van and looked across the street. The mayor stood in the middle of the fire station, surveying the array of photographs now adorning the station's rear wall. "Bailey looks in pretty good shape to me."

"She'll be delighted to hear the disguise is working." Elena took hold of his free hand. "Oh, and the governor's late."

"Outstanding."

"Exactly what Mom said. Only with more volume." Elena tugged on his hand. "Come on, sport. There are things to do and people to yell at."

"One second." Dillon surveyed the three segments that made up the growing street carnival. The smallest was also the quietest. And by far the most orderly. Inside the fire station, a stern-faced mayor oversaw a quietly cheerful team laying out trestle tables, benches, and folding chairs carried over from the town hall. In one corner of the fire station's rear wall, alongside Olivia's pictorial display, now stood a podium, mikes, and loudspeakers. Dillon wanted to rush over, embrace Bailey again, tell her what an incredible job she was doing. All that.

But he couldn't. Because the other two segments shared an element that could be summed up in just one word.

Party.

Elena demanded, "Why are we standing here?"

"I'm trying to find where I can help out." Dillon swept his free hand over the noisy scene. "It looks to me like people are pretty much getting on with their jobs."

Elena lifted up on her tiptoes and squinted. "You ask me, the zebras and hippos have taken control of the circus."

Dillon's response was cut off by Claire shouldering

through the crowd, followed by a grinning Arnaud. Claire planted fists on hips and demanded, "What's the big idea?"

"About what?" Dillon sketched a wave. "Hi, Arnaud."

"Don't mind me. I'm just the innocent bystander here," Arnaud replied.

"You and me both," Elena said.

Claire asked, "Why weren't we invited to help out with this gig?"

"Nobody invited anyone. This all just sort of happened."

"Huh." She glared at Elena. "Have you ever in your entire life heard such a lame excuse?"

"Thinking."

"I've got six turkeys ready to come out of the oven," Claire announced.

Arnaud cleared his throat. "Actually, I'm the one—"

"Don't you start." To Dillon, "I called Bailey an hour ago. She claims you're directing traffic. So direct."

It was Elena who suggested, "Turkey tacos."

The three adults stared at her. Dillon said, "That's actually a very good idea."

"California fast food, Christmas style," Elena said.

Claire looked at her husband, who said, "Works for me."

Claire said, "We can whip up some sides of slaw and potato salad."

"I can," Arnaud replied. "You can't boil water."

Dillon pointed to the fire station. "Set up your station in the chief's office. Get ready to feed the governor's crew and all the Miramar biggies."

"Don't forget Santa," Elena said, offering them a happy shrug. "What can I tell you. I'm still ten."

38

In the end, Dillon joined Porter and Charlie Hurst. The two chiefs and numerous volunteers laid out cables from the generators, three of which now throbbed merrily under the guidance of a grinning power-company engineer. They worked hard, sweated buckets, and raced against the ticking clock. Gleason was in charge of another merry band of volunteers, who gradually reduced the massive pile of lawn ornaments.

Elena played Dillon's runner throughout.

An hour and a half later, Bailey marched over and said, "I'm here to collect my wayward daughter."

Dillon and Elena said it together. "Awww."

Bailey looked from one to the other. "Apparently I've been transported to some alternate dimension."

Gleason and Charlie Hurst walked over, sweating and grinning. Charlie said, "Somebody point me toward the bar."

"No bar," Bailey said. "Nix on booze of any shape, form, grape, grain, a total ban. The last thing we need is to greet our guests with a riot."

Porter had sidled up as well. "Probably a good idea, at least until the governor leaves."

Bailey asked, "Just wondering, has anybody checked to see if all these lights will actually turn on?"

"Oh, right." Charlie wiped his face with an oil-stained rag. "We'll get around to that by tomorrow, no problem."

"That was not funny in the extreme," Bailey replied.

"Don't mess with Mayor Mom," Elena warned. "She might explode."

Dillon said, "We've done a running test. Everything checks out."

Gleason surveyed the array of lawn ornaments that now stretched along both sides of the lane, climbed the light poles, and framed the town hall. "Exactly how many reindeers does one Santa need?"

"It's okay to have extras," Elena said, "you know, in case some get lost in that candy cane forest growing across the street."

Porter said, "I don't recall ever reading about six dozen bunny rabbits playing a role in the Christmas story."

"That's nothing." Gleason pointed to the town hall's roofline. "Get a load of the glow-in-the-dark pilgrims with their tame turkeys getting ready to take down the angel. That's a felony in the making."

Elena said, "You two really need to get out more."

"The governor's on approach," Bailey announced. "Porter, you and me and the other bigwigs need to go pretend we're glad to see him."

"Not me," Charlie replied. "Me and Dillon and these eleventy-seven volunteers are going to light up the town."

"Whatever works." Bailey reached over, hugged her daughter. "Excuse me while I requisition this elf. The rest of you, pretend like you know what you're doing."

Dillon and the others waved as Bailey and her daughter departed in the police chief's ride, followed by a slow parade of vehicles—two more police cars, Berto's Tahoe, Emilia's Cadillac SUV, a power company bus for the press. When the parade of vehicles rounded the corner and the sirens dimmed, Dillon asked the fire chief, "Shouldn't you be with them?"

"Politicians give me hives."

"You and Mayor Bailey get along well enough."

"Yeah, well, there are exceptions to every rule." Charlie offered him a sweaty grin. "Speaking of getting along with the mayor."

"You can finish that thought, or you can have me

help get this rig up and running," Dillon replied. "Your choice."

Twenty minutes later he paused again when a volunteer brought coffee and more doughnuts. As he munched, Dillon inspected the cables running around the town hall. But mostly it was a good moment for a gut check. And what Dillon felt just then was how much he liked being exactly where he was.

As he started back across the street, his phone pinged. Dillon checked the screen, and read a text from Elena. **Ready for G-Day?**

G-Day. Cute. And yes.

Really, really ready?

Dillon turned as the crowd lining both sides of the street broke into a cheer. Section by section, the lights came on. He texted, **Wow.**

Wow good or wow bad? This is your unpaid assistant elf. I can be discreet. But it will cost you.

Elena, this looks incredible.

So I can tell Mayor Mom the generators are working?

At that very moment, the band on the town hall's front porch began playing. Their first number was a powerful rendition of "Rock Around the Clock."

The crowd clearly loved having another reason to cheer.

Dillon surveyed the illuminated street, the smiles, the laughter, the children going nuts, the families holding the littlest ones up high enough to see it all.

His phone pinged. **HELLO???**

He texted back, **Wrong question.**

Okay, I'm game. What should her royal majesty the grand high poohbah of Miramar be asking?

Dillon replied, **Are we having fun yet? And the answer is a total unqualified yes.**

A longish pause, then, **This is me laughing.**

A faint drumming lifted faces, up and down the street. As the approaching helicopter's noise grew in volume, Elena texted, **Here comes trouble.**

We're ready at this end, Dillon texted back. **I think.**

The drumming grew louder still, then went quiet.

Elena texted, **Eagle has landed.**

Dillon headed back to what had formerly been a vacant lot and was now a hive of last-minute preparations. Charlie greeted him with, "What had you working your phone?"

"I was busy flirting with a ten-year-old." Dillon pointed toward the Pacific. "They're here."

Of all the smiles filling the scene, Charlie's was by far the grandest. "Let's hope they make it into town before all the fuses blow."

39

The governor's security detail and Boyd Harrow, his chief of staff, were first off the helicopter. Boyd shook Bailey's hand, then made some comment that had the mayor pointing in Olivia's direction.

Boyd signaled to the security, who took up station by the chopper's stairs as the governor appeared. Victor Lowell was a politician on the rise, young for such a position, and every inch the statesman. His speech at the previous national convention had many talking about him as a future president.

Following the governor was what to Olivia looked like a circus clown act, only better dressed. An unlikely number of people piled out, many carrying sound and video equipment.

"Olivia Greer? Hi. Boyd Harrow. Mayor Long says you're the lady to advise on our photo op." He surveyed the setting with a doubtful frown. "She also said that was why you suggested we land here."

Their vehicles all had headlights pointed at the fractured parking area. The lot and the partly destroyed walkway stood about forty feet above the beach. The rocky promontory had been chewed away, so that in the afternoon's gathering shadows, the drop looked precipitous.

Olivia pointed down the shore. "The ocean walk is at the heart of our community. See those four bridges?"

"What's left of them."

Shadows from the westering sun cast the damage in skeletal definition. "You could have the mayor and the governor walk past one."

"The road would be a safer bet. If the governor falls on the descent, that's the photo you'll see on every Christmas front page."

"There are steps back where the lot meets the road," Bailey replied. "And if he walks the road, the pictures will show him viewing the damage from a safe height."

"Good point." Boyd wheeled about. "Let's get this show on the beach."

Olivia stayed well back as the crowd descended. Porter and his officers illuminated their way with portable spots. Counting Bailey and Elena and the governor's security, they numbered seventeen—far too many for Olivia to frame in any kind of meaningful shot. Olivia followed about fifty paces behind, half hoping for the photo she thought just might happen.

So many grand things were at work in this small moment. She had been welcomed home with such unexpected warmth. Her reentry had been made almost complete by these professional opportunities. Some of which had resulted in the best work she had ever done. And tomorrow, Christmas Day, she would move into her temporary new home, shared with the man who had once broken her heart. And who now was her dearest friend.

A pair of winged gulls wrote their feathered script into the blue-gold sky overhead. The tangy scent of ocean and salt and seaweed filled her being. Time slowed as she found an ideal spot and knelt where the shadows concealed her presence. Olivia felt so weightless she could almost join the seabirds in their soaring dance.

She had returned to Miramar a different person. There was no other explanation for how this moment, in this place, left her feeling so, well . . .

Complete.

And at that precise moment, the shot Olivia had been hoping for came together.

Governor Lowell was known as both personable and courteous, even by his opponents. His security knew their man and their job. Soon as the requisite photo op was completed, they shepherded the group back toward the waiting vehicles. Leaving the governor temporarily on his own, except for the one local photographer, shadowed by the westering sun, who knelt motionless.

Olivia waited and watched as . . .

Governor Lowell walked toward two couples who had not joined the town's festivities. They dragged wood salvaged from the sea and stacked it against the stone-lined elevation. He shook hands and listened as they explained how salt-treated timber, once fully dried out, became hard as iron. How these locals loved their fairylike boardwalk and wanted to be part of its reconstruction. Olivia knew all this because she had stood where the governor was now.

She waited.

The governor listened intently as the townspeople shared their determination to help renovate their beloved Miramar.

The town had known massive back-to-back fire seasons. This had been followed by floods and mudslides and weeks of hurricane-force winds. All of which had been preceded by a viral plague.

If ever a California settlement held the ability to play the phoenix, and rise from the central coast's version of the apocalypse, it was Miramar.

Behind her, the governor's entourage complained loudly as they scrambled up the rubble-strewn ledge, equipment in hand. The in-front-of-the-camera types moaned over the damage to their shoes, pants, nails, whatever. She remained intent, waiting, focused, until it happened.

The descending sun touched the western hills' leading rim. A veil of golden fire spread overhead, a brilliant display of California dusk. The governor chose that moment to shake another hand and say something that brought smiles to all the weary faces.

The soon-to-be-rebuilt walkway formed a softly glowing backdrop. Olivia felt the wet chill soak her legs from the knees down and did not care. She breathed the iodine-spiced air. Her heart sang with the gulls. As she shot her photographs, Olivia softly chanted one word. Over and over.

Perfect.

40

Forty minutes later, Elena texted that the governor's entourage was on its way. Their work connecting the generators was almost done, and only now did Dillon have time to regret his stained and sweaty state. He was tempted to go back and shower and change.

As in, return to the jail.

Where he was about to spend Christmas Eve.

Of course, some of his former investors would no doubt cheer the news.

Charlie Hurst stepped up beside him and demanded, "What's got you taking a bite from a spoiled pickle?"

Dillon opted to stow away his mental baggage and reply, "I was thinking maybe I should run back and shower."

"Not a chance."

"I'm filthy."

"Join the club. The mayor's got more important

things to worry about than your smelly state. Now come help me change."

The cottage that had once been Olivia's home now possessed its own set of decorative lights. Two of their tallest candy canes flanked the front door. Dillon entered and stood between a pair of Christmas trees as Charlie pulled a red velvet Santa suit from a battered canvas satchel. Charlie lay the jacket on the high-backed chair now occupying the cottage's front room and declared, "This thing keeps getting tighter every year."

Charlie stripped off his boots and trousers, struggled into the pants, then stopped when the open zipper formed a six-inch V-shaped gap. "Uh-oh."

"Not good," Dillon agreed.

"Okay, that's it." Charlie shucked off the trousers and pulled his own back into place. "You try."

"Me? No way."

"Get your sorry Christmas carcass over here and strip."

"Charlie, there's no way I'm playing Santa."

"Oh, really." He held out the velvet trousers. "You think it'd be better for me to greet the kiddies and their parents with my pants open for business?"

"There's got to be somebody else."

"We don't have time for this." He shook the trousers. "Say, ho ho ho."

"Ho ho ho."

"Okay, that was pretty lame. Do it again, only this time add some salsa."

"Ho ho ho."

"Louder!"

"Ho ho ho!"

"Okay, you're hired." Charlie tossed him the pants. "Now get dressed."

Porter drove the lead vehicle and took it slow up Ocean Avenue. The street was illuminated by a few feebly glowing streetlights. The procession's solemn air was emphasized by how empty the town appeared. Not a soul walked the sidewalks, no cars, no lights in all the buildings they passed.

One of the governor's security detail sat next to the police chief. Olivia shared the rear seat with Ransom Bates. The state auditor was both glum and cross, his expression saying exactly what he thought of spending his Christmas Eve in Miramar.

The security was a stocky woman with a voice almost as deep as Porter's. "Looks like a ghost town."

The chief pointed through the front windshield at the glow illuminating the horizon. "You'll meet the locals soon enough."

She leaned forward and squinted. "Tell me that's not a riot."

Porter actually laughed. "This is a Christmas festival, Miramar style."

The agent was clearly displeased. "I didn't see any memo about your hosting a party for the governor."

"This sort of happened at the last minute. Not to mention how we only heard about your visit yesterday." Porter smiled at her. "We'll do our best to make you feel welcome."

As they passed the shuttered Castaways and entered the first block illuminated by Christmas lights, their progress was halted by noisy, happy, jostling crowds. Porter announced, "We'll need to hoof it from here."

The agent looked doubtful. "You're sure it's safe?"

"Don't you worry." Porter pulled into the empty fire lane. "Me and my team, we'll have your back."

As they rose from the vehicles, Olivia decided it was a night made for drama. Behind her, the darkened blocks of Ocean Avenue had been stripped of decorations. A few strands of tinsel still drifted from the lampposts. Otherwise nothing stirred.

The road up ahead was something else entirely. Their way was illuminated by every imaginable form of lawn ornament, strung in happy abandon from telephone poles, shop fronts, bushes, trees. The governor's security were mildly freaked as they pressed forward. This was, after all, California. But it was also Christmas Eve. In Miramar. A block later, surrounded by good-natured throngs, the governor finally told his guard detail to hang back and keep cool. Then he began working the crowd. The journalists and television crews managed to get their lights on and cameras focused as . . .

Word spread that Governor Lowell was among them. People shouted hellos, called and yelled messages no one bothered to hear, held out babies and young children for him to greet, flashed a million selfies. All in all, it was as warm and easygoing a welcome as any politician could hope for.

Olivia saw how both the governor and his team were confused, uncertain. They had come to inspect and meet officials of a storm-damaged town in serious need of help. Instead, they were swept up, carried along, and invited to join the celebration.

The streetlights were out here as well, but their poles were festooned with baubles and lights connected to the softly thrumming generators. The road was lined with a forest of illuminated lawn ornaments— tree-size candy canes, reindeers, mangers, mock Christmas trees, Santas, elves, angels galore. Yet more lights climbed the town hall's front, illuminating the band playing a jazzy rendition of Santa coming to town.

Then the crowd parted, and Olivia caught sight of her cottage.

The home she grew up in and fought so hard to escape was transformed. Of the house itself there appeared to be nothing left. Instead, there before her stood a Christmas cottage made up exclusively of light. And laughter. And great good cheer.

Angels and sleighs and reindeer and elves crowded for space along the roof. Her former home was now the centerpiece, the heart to this joyous moment. The storm had passed, and the town was swept into a sweet hour of celebration. Welcoming Miramar into a season of hope.

Her cottage, Olivia decided, had been made for this very moment.

Abruptly the Christmas lights, Miramar's happy clan, the music, coalesced into a certainty that her mother was close at hand. Olivia could almost hear her humming along with the band playing carols, sharing in this miracle.

Then Dillon appeared in her cottage doorway.

He was dressed in an ill-fitting Santa suit and held a child of perhaps three or four. The girl wore Dillon's red cap and squealed with laughter. Charlie Hurst and Gleason stood to either side of the doorway. They pretended to keep a mob of kids and their parents in an orderly line. But the two men were laughing too hard for the children to pay them any mind.

Then Dillon spotted Olivia. He slipped the hat back on his head, handed the girl to her giggling parents, then lifted his arms in the air and shouted, *"HO HO HO!"*

The crowd yelled back to him. Hundreds of voices, like they had spent weeks readying for this very moment. Ho ho ho.

Olivia realized the mayor and her daughter had stepped up beside her. Elena pointed to Dillon and said, "I know what I want for Christmas."

Bailey took hold of Elena's hand. "Come on, kiddo. Let's go make Santa's day." To Olivia, "Go show the governor your work. I'll be with you directly."

Watching Bailey and Elena march toward him, Dillon felt like all the Christmases he'd ever known were crystallizing into this grand instant. He stepped through the doorway, snagged Gleason, passed him the red hat, and said, "Tag, you're it."

Dillon moved away before Gleason could object, and was ready when the two ladies joined him. Bailey wrapped her arms around his neck, and Elena hugged the two of them. Dillon's own embrace was strengthened by his Christmas wish. He breathed the heady aromas of love and spoke his wish aloud: "I want this union to be forever forged."

"Wow," Elena said. "Chills."

"Good," Bailey said. "I like having something we can agree on."

"Something important," Elena said. "Something vital."

They stood there a long moment, awash in music and laughter and many voices singing off-key. Finally Dillon asked, "Aren't you supposed to be hosting the governor?"

"He's a big boy," Bailey replied. "He can take care of himself for three minutes."

"Olivia's making sure he doesn't get lost," Elena said.

Just the same, Bailey gently pried herself free. "Does Santa get hungry?"

"This one sure does."

They started toward the fire station, Dillon holding hands with Bailey on one side and Elena on the other. Being linked as a threesome made for heavy going through the crowd, but Dillon did not mind and clearly the ladies felt the same. Across the street, the band played a jazzy rendition of "I'll Be Home for Christmas." The two singers, both women, were excellent. The crowd cheered, sang along, kissed, danced.

The firehouse was a hive of good cheer. Elena released him long enough to snag three tacos. As they ate, they shifted toward the rear wall and took up station a few steps removed from where Porter and Olivia led the governor's group. Both Victor Lowell and his number two appeared fascinated by what was on display. Even the auditor, Ransom Bates, lost some of his sour cast. Olivia only spoke if the governor or Boyd said something. Otherwise she and Porter let the photographs do the talking.

The pictures were a collage that rendered Miramar into a colorful and glorious before-and-after display.

When Dillon stepped before the sea wall medley, he breathed a soft, *wow*.

Elena said, "I know, right?"

He took a step back, trying to absorb the entire display at once. "It's like . . ."

"She's captured the whole town," Elena said.

"These aren't just pictures," Bailey agreed. "They reveal . . ."

"The town's hidden heart," Elena said.

Dillon asked, "Do you often put words in other people's mouths?"

"Only when she's at her most irritating," Bailey replied.

"Just the same, it's true." Dillon could see Olivia's future there on the wall, clear as a roadmap to what she would soon become.

Bailey finished her taco, carefully wiped her fingers and mouth, then clung to him. One arm was wrapped firmly around Dillon's waist, the other gripped his arm, while her head rested in the point where his shoulder met his neck. A spot, Dillon decided, that was made for her. A place that had been empty for far too long.

Elena clung to his free hand and bounced on her toes, so excited and happy that she was, for this one moment, still a child.

Another step, another set of images. Dillon felt as if the two ladies, the photographs, and the entire moment served as a mirror. He saw anew his younger version, and recalled how hard he had fought to break free. The Dillon who had done his best to carve a niche in a fiercely competitive world. And he had succeeded. Until he failed. And that had brought him back to Miramar, where he'd hoped for nothing more than a chance to catch his breath. *Healing* was a word he had dared not use.

And look what this Christmas had brought him.

Purpose. Hope. A tomorrow. And so much more besides.

Dillon told them, "It's good to be home."